FOOLISH MERCY

The mounted Blackfoot lowered his lance and charged. Hawk didn't want to kill him, just warn him off, so he lifted the rifle and fired over his head. The Indian ducked. That was all the edge Hawk needed.

Darting in close, Hawk grabbed the lance just behind the steel point, and yanked the warrior off his pony. The Blackfoot landed on his back, rolled away, then leaped to his feet. Drawing his knife, he charged. Hawk reached behind his neck. In one lightning motion, he unsheathed his throwing knife and sent it slamming into the Indian's chest.

The Blackfoot fell to one knee. The blade had struck a rib, not deep enough to be fatal. The Indian flung the knife contemptuously back at Hawk. Then he caught his pony's reins and mounted.

Fist raised, he rode off. "Black Feather will meet Golden Hawk again!" he cried.

Golden Hawk had made the worst mistake he could in a land where the first rule was kill or be killed . . .

D1209753

GOLDEN HAWK 6

SCALPER'S TRAIL

Will C. Knott

A SIGNET BOOK

NEW AMERICAN LIBRARY

PUBLISHER'S NOTE

This book is a work of fiction. Names, characters, places, and incidents either are the product of the author's imagination or are used fictitiously, and any resemblance to actual persons, living or dead, events, or locales is entirely coincidental.

Copyright © 1987 by Will C. Knott

SIGNET TRADEMARK REG. U.S. PAT. OFF. AND FOREIGN COUNTRIES REGISTERED TRADEMARK—MARCA REGISTRADA HECHO EN CHICAGO, U.S.A.

SIGNET, SIGNET CLASSIC, MENTOR, ONYX, PLUME, MERIDIAN and NAL BOOKS are published by NAL PENGUIN INC., 1633 Broadway, New York, New York 10019

First Printing, December, 1987

1 2 3 4 5 6 7 8 9

PRINTED IN THE UNITED STATES OF AMERICA

GOLDEN HAWK

A quiet stream under the Comanche moon . . . leaping savages . . . knives flashing in the firelight . . . brutal, shameful death . . .

Ripped from the bosom of their slain parents and carried off by the raiding Comanches, Jed Thompson and his sister can never forget that hellish night under the glare of the Comanche moon, seared into their memories forever.

Years later, his vengeance slaked, pursued relentlessly by his past Comanche brothers, Jed is Golden Hawk. Half Comanche, half white man. A legend in his time, an awesome nemesis to some—a bulwark and a refuge to any man or woman lost in the terror of that raw, savage land.

— Prologue —

Hawk was not sure what he saw. And then he was. Through the trees the bright flicker of a campfire beckoned. Ready to make his own camp, Hawk paused. The campfire might mean a chance to light up his pipe and enjoy the company of another mountain man. Or it could be the camp of a Blackfoot warrior eager for a white man's scalp, in which case Hawk would be wise to move on farther upstream. Glancing back at his dun to make sure it was tethered securely, he glided swiftly into the timber.

Just before he reached the clearing in which the campfire blazed, he heard a hard, snarling voice followed by a scuffle. A shot rang out. As Hawk emerged from the timber a moment later, he saw a trapper on the other side of the campfire transferring plews from an Indian's pony to his own. A Blackfoot Indian was sprawled facedown over the fire, the stench of burning flesh filling the night air.

Dashing to the fire, Hawk grabbed the Indian by

the shoulder and dragged him off the fire, noting as he did the bullet wound high on the left side of the Indian's chest. Turning then to face the trapper, Hawk found himself looking into the muzzle of a long Kentucky rifle.

The trapper's eyes were red-rimmed and burned with a fierce, mad light. Spittle leaked out of one corner of his mouth. He chuckled. "You come to help me load up this Blackfoot's pelts, have you, mister?"

"No need for you to wave that rifle at me."

"How do I know you ain't a partner of this here redskin?"

"Blackfoot and I don't mix all that easy."

The trapper relaxed some. "Then why in hell did you pull him off the fire?"

"I don't like the smell of burning flesh. Not when it's human, that is."

The trapper smirked and licked his lips. "Hell! Who says a Blackfoot's human?"

Hawk did not answer.

"Back off now while I look you over."

But Hawk remained where he was, looming silently beside the fire. He was better than six feet tall, with a golden shock of hair reaching to his broad, powerful shoulders. His sun-bronzed face was intent, watchful, his powerful glance catching the trapper's nervously shifting eyes and holding them. His sharp beak of a nose reminded most men of a hawk—a very alert hawk, ready to pounce. Wearing a quilted buckskin shirt and trousers, and doeskin moccasins instead of riding boots, he was dressed more like an Indian than a white man.

Under the pressure of Hawk's quiet menace, the trapper lost some of his bravado and took a hesitant step back, lowering his rifle as he did so. Hawk was astonished at the man's ugliness. His nose had no bridge to it and sat flat on his face, like the snout of a pig. A white scar ran from under his left eye to the corner of his mouth. Shorter than Hawk, he had thinning black hair. His clothes were in tatters and he stank worse than a skunk in heat.

Hawk took a step toward the man, intending to rip the rifle from his grasp. "This Blackfoot's liable to take it unkindly if you ride off with his goods," Hawk reminded him. "Maybe you better leave them here."

The trapper lifted the rifle again. "You think I mind what that stinking heathen thinks?" the trapper snarled, pure madness flaring in his eyes. "I say cast them all into the fires of hell! Let the bastards burn! Every damn one of 'em!"

He took a quick step back, turned, and swung into his saddle, winding his packhorse's lines about his saddle horn as he did so. Hawk was about to reach up and pull him off the horse when he heard a muffled cry behind him.

He turned. The Indian had regained consciousness. On his feet now, he charged Hawk. Plowing furiously into him, he drove Hawk back against the trapper's horse. As the animal shied away, then reared, Hawk tried to deal with the infuriated Blackfoot. They grappled for a moment and Hawk felt himself stumbling backward across the fire. His left foot caught a blazing stick of firewood. He sprawled to the ground, the Blackfoot landing on top of him.

At that moment Hawk heard the trapper spur his horse across the small meadow.

The Blackfoot leaped to his feet and raced desperately after the trapper. Snatching up his rifle, Hawk watched the two vanish into the darkness and for a moment considered going after them. Then, with a weary shrug, he turned his back on them, skirted the campfire, and returned through the timber to his waiting dun. Untying it, he rode on upstream for a good mile or so, intent on putting as much distance as possible between him and those two. He found a spot to his liking and made his camp.

He had just returned from the East—a town near Boston—where he had spent a few months with his sister Annabelle and her husband Captain Merriwether. He was now on his way from Fort Union to overtake Joe Meek, who was guiding a wagon train through the mountains to Oregon. Hawk would rather have gone straight on to his cabin on the Snake—and to Raven Eyes, the Crow woman he hoped would be waiting for him—but Joe Meek had insisted that he needed Hawk as a guide through Blackfoot country, and Hawk had not seen how he could deny his old friend. This chore would take less than a month, Joe Meek had promised, and long before the snow flew, Hawk would be back on the Snake.

It was late and Hawk was weary. He was also ravenous. He threw a few chunks of jerky and salt pork into his fry pan and set it over the flames. The smell of it frying set his mouth to watering, and he ate it almost before it was ready, wolfing down the meal like a starved beast.

Drowsy, he lit his pipe and sat down a small distance from the fire. Leaning his back against a tree, he saw in his mind's eye the enraged Blackfoot chasing the crazed trapper into the dark timber. Shaking his head, he leaned his head back against the tree and allowed his heavy lids to close for just a moment.

He came awake with a start. It was light. Early morning mists were still hovering close to the ground and over the surface of the stream in front of him. He had slept through the night without the warmth of his bedroll about him and his limbs were stiff. Something had awakened him. What?

Then he heard the steady drumbeat of galloping hooves.

He reached for his rifle and stood up to see the wounded Blackfoot he had saved the night before galloping across the meadow toward him. As the mists parted for him, the Indian's face became clearer and Hawk saw the black war paint running in parallel streaks across his forehead and down his cheeks. Like a demon charging from the fires of hell, he was coming straight for Hawk.

In Blackfoot, Hawk yelled, "You damn fool Indian! I was only tryin' to help you!"

The Blackfoot ignored Hawk's words, pulled up about fifty yards away, and began circling Hawk, daring Hawk to fire on him. The Indian's chest was raw where the campfire's flames had roasted it, and Hawk could see the entry wound high on his right shoulder. The Blackfoot had circled it with yellow war paint and sent lines in red ocher radiating out from its center.

"Go back!" Hawk called out to him in Blackfoot. "I am not your enemy. I'm the one who pulled you off that fire!"

"Huh!" the Indian taunted, still circling. "Why should Black Feather believe Golden Hawk." He smiled then, his even white teeth gleaming against his blackened face. "Soon Golden Hawk's scalp will hang from Black Feather's scalp pole!"

There was nothing Hawk could do or say, he realized. The Blackfoot was convinced he and the trapper had been working together.

Nudging his pony's right flank with his thigh, the Indian lowered his lance and charged Hawk. Hawk did not want to kill this Indian, just warn him off. Waiting until the Blackfoot was almost on him, Hawk lifted the rifle barrel slightly and fired over his head. Instinctively, the Indian ducked lower in the saddle.

This was all the edge Hawk needed.

Darting in close to the charging horse and rider, he grabbed the Blackfoot's lance just behind the steel point with his left hand and with his right grabbed the shaft farther down. Digging his feet in securely, he yanked the warrior off his pony. Landing on his back a few feet from Hawk, the Blackfoot rolled swiftly away, then leaped to his feet. Drawing his knife, he charged. Hawk reached behind his neck. In one swift, lightning-like motion, he unsheathed his throwing-knife and sent it at the charging Indian. The blade slammed into his chest.

The Blackfoot halted, then fell to one knee. The blade had struck a rib and was not nearly deep enough to be fatal. The Indian withdrew the knife and flung it contemptuously back at Hawk. His well-trained pony was galloping back to him. Reaching back, he caught the reins and mounted up.

Fist raised, he rode off. "Black Feather will meet Golden Hawk again!" he cried.

Hawk sighed wearily and picked up his bloody knife. Watching the Blackfoot vanish back into the morning mists, Hawk did not doubt they would meet again.

Only next time, Hawk would shoot to kill.

— Chapter One —

As soon as news of the nearby buffalo herd reached the wagons, Joe Meek and Hawk saddled up and set out to do what they could to fill the wagon train's larder. Accompanying them was young Tommy Fitzpatrick, whose job it would be to ride back to the wagons to fetch men to butcher the buffalo and mules to take the dressed meat back to the wagons.

They were in Blackfoot country, and whatever buffalo they cut down would, by right, belong to the people of that savage confederacy. Nevertheless, the train's captain, Henry Shaw, was anxious to obtain as much fresh meat as possible before the wagons reached the mountains. There was another reason as well—the buffalo meat itself. For weeks they had had to be satisfied with venison, salt pork, and jerky. Now would come feast time. Rich, tender, and fiberless, buffalo was the most succulent meat of all.

They had ridden little more than a mile when they crested a low ridge and saw below them a vast herd of buffalo. So crowded were the buffalo that clear to the distant horizon the herd resembled one vast, humped carpet. Closer, on the river's southern bank, the buffalo were less densely packed, and everywhere Hawk and Joe Meek looked, small bands of buffalo were grazing on the short, succulent grama grasses that carpeted the prairie. Patches of dust rose where some of the shaggy beasts rolled about on the ground, and here and there a battle was going forward among the bulls as the rutting season approached. They could hear the bulls bellowing hoarsely.

For a while Hawk and Joe Meek were content to sit on their horses and watch. Then they rode on down the far side of the ridge, heading toward a hollow that would take them to the rutted plain stretching alongside this side of the river, where they hoped to corral one of the smaller bands. A half mile or so from the riverbank, they spotted a small bunch—three cows and a young bull—grazing at the head of a wooded coulee. It was typical of buffalo in the open to graze in country pocked with deep ravines or narrow wooded coulees, the kind of country that made it difficult for horses to follow them.

Looking over the four buffalo, Joe Meek was pleased. "All we have to do is drive them into that coulee."

"Hell, Joe," Hawk protested. "It's too damn close in there."

"Who said we'd go in after them? I'll circle around from the other side and wait for 'em. You just drive them at that coulee. I'll wait for them at the entrance. It'll be like shootin' fish in a barrel."

"I can shoot," piped up Tommy. "I brought my rifle."

The two men turned to look at the freckled, tow-headed youngster. He was barely eleven and father-less, but he could ride better than most men, and his greatest pleasure, it seemed, was to stick with the older men to listen and help out when need be. He was all-fired anxious to grow up and be a man, it seemed.

"Keep that rifle of yours quiet," Joe Meek told him, "and stay back and wave your saddle blanket when we tell you to, and light out if that bull comes at you. You hear me, son?"

"Yes sir."

Tommy stayed close behind as Hawk and Joe Meek headed toward the buffalo. Pulling up in a draw upwind of the great, shaggy beasts, the two men dismounted and crept up the side of the draw to take a closer look at them. They were about four hundred yards away, unaware as yet of their ap-proach, placidly feeding on the grama. The young bull had lost his winter coat, but his appearance was formidable enough. He looked about ten years old and probably weighed nearly a ton. Approach-ing his prime, he was close to six feet tall at the shoulders and from muzzle to rump at least ten feet long. The cows seemed less formidable in ap-pearance; but they were big and strong enough to intimidate any man on horseback.

Something alarmed the bull. He swung around, his head upraised as he tried to catch their scent, his narrow, sticklike legs moving him about with surprising nimbleness. Behind him, the cows backed up, their hind ends pointing at the coulee entrance.

"See that," whispered Joe Meek. "They'll go for the coulee first thing."

"Go on. Get going."

Scrambling back down the draw, Joe Meek leaped astride his horse and rode off, keeping in the draw. Hawk tightened his saddle girth, then checked his rifle's load and that of his big Colt before mounting up. He turned to Tommy and saw that he already had his saddle blanket in his hand.

"When I wave my hat," Hawk told the boy, "you start for the buffalo and wave your blanket. Make as much noise as you can. Keep them from cutting back this way. Think you can manage that?"

"Sure, Mr. Hawk."

It was the first time Tommy had ever addressed him in that manner and Hawk made a mental note to speak to him about it later. When he had signed on as scout, he had used his given name, Jed Thompson. Turning back around in his saddle, Hawk dug his heels into his mount's side and charged up out of the coulee, waving his hat and crying out like a Comanche. Instantly the three cows wheeled and made for the coulee—just as Joe Meek had predicted.

The bull, however, was not going to be intimidated. Pawing the ground, he lashed his tail, lowered his head, and charged. Hawk had no difficulty avoiding the first rush, but when he tried to cut after the fleeing cows, the enraged harem master took after Hawk with a speed that astonished and dismayed him. He flung his horse around just in time to avoid the bull's horns. The bull skipped nimbly about to come at him again. Hawk raised his rifle and, sighting along the barrel, aimed at the beast's brisket and fired.

He saw a puff of dust explode where the bullet entered, but the bull only shook his head at Hawk, as if to say he was *not* pleased. Then he came at Hawk again, more slowly perhaps, but just as determined. Hawk poured powder into the rifle's muzzle in what he hoped was a double charge and spat a ball down the barrel after it. Pounding the rifle butt on the saddle to seat the bullet, he flung it up swiftly and fired point-blank at the charging bull. The bullet went into the buffalo's right eye and appeared to explode inside his skull. And still the bull did not go down. Lumbering eerily past Hawk, he swung blindly around and charged off.

Hawk would have let him go, but he saw Tommy on the ground directly in the bull's path, his horse thrashing on the ground beside him. Hauling his horse around, Hawk overtook the bull, emptying his revolver into the great, lumbering beast's back. Every bullet raised dust on the beast's pelt; but incredibly, the bull kept moving, heading directly at Tommy.

"Get down, Tommy!" Hawk yelled.

Obediently, Tommy flung himself into a shallow depression behind the horse. Then Hawk groaned as he saw Tommy's rifle poke up, the muzzle aimed at the bull.

Again Hawk reloaded his rifle, swung around in front of the buffalo, and fired into its skull. But this time the thick cover of coarse, matted hair that covered the bull's skull deflected the bullet. As Hawk swept past the bull, he heard Tommy fire his rifle. Turning in his saddle, he saw Tommy throw down his rifle and break into the open, fleeing in panic from the furious bull. Scrambling frantically over the rutted, stony ground, he fell, then got up, dodged, and would have fallen again if the bull had not caught him with his horn and tossed him over his back. Tommy lay where he struck and the bull circled around to finish the job.

Hawk jumped off his horse and went down on his knee, spat his last round into the rifle's barrel, aimed swiftly, and fired. This time the bull took the round in his heart. Pulling up, he spread his legs to brace himself, reluctant to go down. With blood streaming from his mouth and his tongue protruding, his body rolled like a ship at sea, while his shattered head slowly turned from side to side. Then, as if a tap had been turned on inside the beast, a heavy gout of purple blood gushed from his nostrils, his knees buckled, and with a hoarse gasp, the animal fell over onto his side, his legs, rigid in death, extended.

Hawk raced to Tommy's side. The boy was not conscious. But he was breathing and it seemed regular enough. From behind Hawk came the pound of Joe Meek's horse. The mountain man flung himself from the saddle and crouched beside Tommy.

"Jesus, Hawk. What happened?"

"He was afoot when that bull caught him."

Joe Meek pressed his ear against the boy's chest.

His expression showed immediate relief when he heard the steady pound of the boy's heart. He sat back on his haunches. "He'll be comin' 'round, looks like. Just got the breath knocked out of him."

"I'll go see to his horse," Hawk told him, taking out his revolver.

The horse had stepped into a gopher hole and snapped off his leg. It was in considerable pain. Done thrashing by now, its muzzle was covered with foam and its eyes bulged out of its skull. With each breath came a feeble, wheezing cry. Hawk rested the muzzle of his revolver against its forehead and fired. Hawk looked back at Joe Meek.

"You better get over here!" Joe cried.

When Hawk did, he found Tommy awake, but in considerable pain and his face the color of a bedsheet. Beads of cold sweat stood out on his brow. Joe Meek spoke softly so Tommy would not hear. "Looks like he busted some ribs, and there's a mean gash in his back where that bull's horn took him."

"Got any whiskey, Joe?"

Joe Meek took a flask from his saddle bag and held it to Tommy's lips and commanded the boy to drink it. Tommy did as ordered. Not long after, he passed out, a faint grin on his face.

"What about them three buffalo?" Hawk asked Joe Meek.

"Got all three."

"I'll bring Tommy back and send out the butchers."

Joe Meek nodded. "Tell them to make it fast and bring enough mules. I saw some hungry coyotes circlin'. It won't take long before they go for them carcasses. I'll do my best, but I won't be much good after dark."

Hawk mounted up. With surprising gentleness, Joe Meek lifted the unconscious boy up into Hawk's arms. With a quick wave, Hawk started back to the wagon train.

As Hawk rode down the line of wagons, he caught sight of Tommy's mother standing by her wagon. She was talking to Ma Bounty. From the trek's beginning, Ma and Jake Bounty had kept their wagon close behind the wagon belonging to Tommy's mother. An older couple with no children, they had taken the widow and Tommy under their wing. As a result, the two families had come to be regarded by the other settlers as a single family group.

Glad the widow was with Ma Bounty, Hawk pulled up beside her. Tommy's mother turned, saw Tommy in Hawk's arms, and uttered a small, frightened cry. Jake Bounty hurried over to join his wife. He reached up for Tommy. Hawk gave him to the older man, who held the boy in his arms while his distraught mother peered anxiously down at him. Seeing no wound and smelling the whiskey, she looked at Hawk in utter confusion.

"He reeks of alcohol!" she accused.

"We did that to cut the pain."

Her face went white.

"How bad is he?" Jake asked anxiously.

"Maybe a few cracked ribs. He's got a horn wound in his back that better be looked at."

Nodding grimly, Jake carried the boy over to his

wagon, Tommy's mother clinging anxiously to Tommy's hand as he did so. As soon as Ma Bounty, already in the wagon, helped the boy inside it, Hawk spurred his horse on down the line to see to the waiting men and packhorses.

He was in a hurry. As Joe Meek had warned, the wagon train's butchers had to get to those carcasses before there was nothing left to dress.

Even though the wagon train had not yet reached water, Henry Shaw decided to halt where they were and make camp for the night. What with Tommy's injury and the need to bring in the buffalo meat, the wagon train's captain saw no sense in trying to make it any farther that day. There were twenty-six wagons in the train, and once under way the caravan stretched at least a half mile or so, which meant pulling up this early would be an added chore. But the stock needed rest; too much hurrying wore them down, and since the oxen had already hauled the wagons almost ten miles that day, Shaw was willing to settle for that.

A dry camp, however, was not a pleasant one. The families would have to depend on what remained in the water barrels attached to their wagons. The women complained bitterly to their men—until they were reminded of one of the reasons for the early halt. Fresh meat was on the way! Fresh *buffalo* meat!

Soon, cooking fires sprang up everywhere as the freshly butchered buffalo meat reached the train. A great deal of it was set aside for the long journey that still lay ahead of them, but the rest was quickly divided among the settlers. The best and only way to cook fresh buffalo meat was over an open fire, preferably on a spit. Some of the settlers used sticks or long knives held over the flames, but most families constructed spits resting on forked sticks. As more mules arrived laden with meat, additional fires sprang up, fueling an impromptu celebration. As darkness fell, men took out their whiskey jugs and others their fiddles. Dancing began in the firelight, and many young swains, eager for more serious play, took this opportunity to disappear with their lady friends into the darkness beyond the wagons. Meanwhile, the succulent meat filled the night air with a heady, mouth-watering aroma.

But Hawk was not a part of the celebration and neither was Joe Meek. They were crouched in Jake Bounty's wagon with Tommy's mother, watching while Doc Gurney and Kate Bonner, his confidante and helpmate, bent over Tommy, who was fully awake now, twisting and moaning in pain as the doc swabbed out the wound in Tommy's back. He had already bound Tommy's broken ribs.

He pulled back, finished with the horn wound, and let Kate wrap it with bandages. Tommy closed his eyes, exhausted, and allowed his mother to kiss him on the forehead; then he turned his head and slept. Satisfied there was nothing more they could do, Hawk and Joe Meek dropped lightly from the wagon to the ground. Hawk turned to help the widow, and Doc Gurney and Kate Bonner followed.

"Give the boy plenty of water," Gurney told Tommy's mother. "He needs fluids. Washes out the humors, it does."

"What else doctor?" she asked.

"That's all for now."

"Doc, will Tommy be all right? How badly is he hurt?"

"He's got a few cracked ribs, but they'll mend soon enough. I've bound them securely. Just see to it that he doesn't do any ridin' before he's mended. He might puncture a lung. As for that wound, as I said before, just see to it that he gets plenty of fluids."

"And make sure he rests," said Kate.

"That's right," Gurney agreed. "Plenty of rest. So his body can heal."

Ma Bounty leaned out of the wagon. "You go on and get some rest yourself now, child," she called to Tommy's mother. "We'll watch over the tyke."

"Just be sure to change the bandages," Kate Bonner told Tommy's mother. "Keep them clean."

"Now, now," broke in Gurney. "Stuff and nonsense. There's no need to bother about that."

"Don't listen to him," Kate insisted. "You just be sure to keep them bandages clean."

"If you say so," Tommy's mother replied uncertainly.

As Kate left with the doctor, Tommy's mother turned to Hawk, a frown on her face. "Which one do you think I should believe?"

"Kate, I'm thinkin'," said Hawk.

"I agree," said Joe Meek. Then he turned to Hawk. "See you later. I got business with the captain— and I can smell that buffalo meat from here."

Hawk found himself alone with Tommy's mother

and realized suddenly that he was staring. For better than a month he had been unable to ignore her presence on this wagon train. He had noticed from the beginning the considerable skill and uncommon patience she had exhibited handling her oxen team. She kept her wagon up with the rest. It was always neat and her oxen healthy. She kept herself and the boy clean, doing the work of a man and a woman, and never once went looking for help.

It occurred to Hawk that he had never addressed her by her first name. "I don't want to go on callin' you widow, Melanie. Do you mind if I call you by your first name?"

"Why, Jed, of course not. I was wondering why you were so formal."

"Didn't want to presume."

"Some call you Hawk, don't they?"

"Reckon they do, at that."

"I heard you were part Apache."

"No, I'm not part Apache. I'm from Kentucky, Melanie. My folks were killed by the Comanche, and afterward they brought up my sister and me. They're the ones who named me Hawk."

"Golden Hawk."

"Yes."

"I suppose that's because of your hair," she said, looking at it with glowing eyes. He thought she was going to reach out and stroke it and found himself wishing she would.

Then he thought of Raven Eyes.

"You better get back to your wagon," he told her.

"Yes," she said. "You must forgive me. I am very tired."

Then she glanced past him, at the many fires in front of the wagons. At that moment they both seemed to catch the whiff of roasting beef. At once both of them knew what the other was thinking.

Hawk smiled at Melanie. "Maybe we ought to get some of that buffalo meat," he told her. "Before it's all gone, I mean."

Melanie nodded eagerly. "Until this moment," she admitted, "I had no idea how hungry I was."

From a family that had shamelessly gorged itself, they obtained generous portions of dripping meat and went back to Melanie's wagon, where, their backs to a wagon wheel, they devoured the succulent flesh. When they were done with their feast, Hawk became acutely aware of Melanie's presence beside him as she licked her fingers while glancing boldly at him with her fiery green eyes.

Hawk found himself looking back just as provocatively.

He was not thinking of Raven Eyes any longer. Melanie was just about as fetching a widow as he had come upon in a long, long time. She seldom hid her thick, chestnut hair under a bonnet, and her full, mature bosom apparently hated corsets as much as he did.

Without a word she reached out to him, her hand catching his chin and gently pulling his face close to hers. Leaning close, she kissed him on the lips. It was a long, moist kiss.

Pulling back, she whispered, "Wait here!"

She ran to Ma and Jake Bounty's wagon and climbed inside. She was in there for at least five minutes. Then she hurried back to Hawk through the darkness. "Tommy's sleepin' fine," she told Hawk. "Ma says he has no fever!"

"I'm glad of that, Melanie."

"Come up into the wagon, Jed. Now. If you don't I'll never forgive myself—or you."

He laughed and got to his feet. Taking his hand, she pulled Hawk up. Clambering into the wagon after her, Hawk's eagerness made him clumsy. Melanie did not bother to light a lantern. The wagon's darkness closed about them like a throbbing, passionate womb. In an instant, it seemed, both of them were naked, entwined, clawing, sucking at each other, neither one able to get enough of the other, both of them on fire with a scouring, ravaging need.

As he plunged repeatedly into her moist depths, he thought guiltily of Raven Eyes, groaned inwardly, then surged on, wildly, almost angrily. Under him, Melanie's thighs opened wide as she raised her knees until her ankles were locked behind Hawk's back. She rocked back then as her head began to thrash violently from side to side, her face a tight mask of concentration. Hitting bottom with each stroke, Hawk eased off a bit, fearful of hurting her. But she rose anxiously up to meet his thrusts and grabbed his hair with both her hands.

"All of it! I want it all inside me!"

At once he plunged in deeper than he would have imagined possible.

"Yes yes yes yes yes—oh, yes!" she told him, exploding under him, erupting like a primal force, her legs scissoring him so violently, he found himself gasping.

A muffled cry escaped her, and she flung her hand over her mouth to prevent the cry from reaching the next wagon. For a long, delicious moment she came in a series of wild, slowly subsiding explosions. He kept his own climax back for as long as he could, then surged wildly on, thrusting deep into her and letting himself come. . . .

A moment later, both panting happily like youngsters making out behind a barn, he collapsed forward onto her magnificent breasts, stayed there for a moment, then rolled off her.

Turning to him, she blew a lock of damp hair out of her eyes. "You must forgive me, Jed," she said.

"For what?"

"I acted so . . ."

". . . so human," he finished for her, speaking gently. "I imagine it's been a long time for you, hasn't it?"

She sighed. "Yes. Oh, yes. Too long. Women are not supposed to want such things, I know, but, Jed, I was married for nearly eight years, and . . . well, I'm so glad you understand."

He took her in his arms and hugged her gently, thinking this time of Raven Eyes without pain. As soon as he and Joe Meek got this wagon train through the mountains, Hawk would be on his way back to her.

Melanie's warmth prompted him to pull her closer. Though his cup had been emptied earlier, he realized now it hadn't been a cup at all, but a gallon jug. Gazing deep into Melanie's green eyes, he found no bottom there. Smiling provocatively, she leaned back and waited for him. He bent his head over her and took one firm, incandescent breast in his hand. Drawing it into his mouth, he caressed its rock-hard tip eagerly with his tongue.

Her hands came up and pressed eagerly against the back of his head, then slid down along his spine until they reached his tight buttocks. Still pulling hungrily on her nipples, he let his own big hand move slowly over her full, rounded belly, halting at her thick, coilly nap, thrusting his fingers through it to the pubic mound under it. Probing gently lower, he felt her grow moist under his fingers and she lifted her thighs eagerly to his touch.

"Ah . . ." she sighed, pressing his head deeper into the sweet warmth of her breasts. "Mmmm . . . !"

He exulted in the willing pliancy of her body as her hips moved against the throbbing warmth of his erection as it lay hard against her.

"Now," she whispered urgently. "Please! Now!"

His lips released her breast and he lifted himself slightly. She slid her torso swiftly under him, her legs opening eagerly as he slipped in, the muscles at her entrance closing tightly. Thrusting slowly, languorously, with her lifting to meet every stroke, they made love, moving to a deep, natural rhythm. They had become something more than a man and a woman.

They had become primal forces content to follow a deeper, more universal beat—until at last their fierce need for completion took over, and their pace increased into a kind of silent, yet wondrous struggle. Great, huffing sighs burst from her, but the need for silence prevented her from crying out. This need for concealment gave an impetus, it seemed, to their swift, violent rush as they plunged over the edge in a series of internal detonations that left them both rocking happily in each other's arms at the wild, delicious memory of it.

A sweet drowsiness fell over Hawk. He lay on his back beside her, his chest rising and falling steadily, Melanie's head resting on him. He dug his fingers deep into the luxuriant glory of her thick, sweaty curls. The funky smell of their lovemaking filled the wagon. He dozed for he did not know how long, and when he awakened, Melanie was bent over him, her melonlike breasts swinging close to his face, their nipples astonishingly erect.

"Now I'm really aroused," she told him, a mischievous light in her green eyes. "You have awakened me fully, Jed!"

Swiftly she climbed onto him, resting a knee alongside each of Hawk's hipbones. She toyed with his moist erection, guiding herself onto it with gentle fingers. As she dropped her pelvis, taking him in deep, then sucking him in still deeper, he offered no protest and allowed her to have her way with him.

She began to move rapidly up and down as if she were riding a horse. Grunting eagerly with each forward thrust, she leaned forward and let her nipples swing across Hawk's face. Lifting his head slightly, he closed his lips around one of her nipples and hung on. She went a little wild then, bucking back and forth with a fury that set off a spark deep in his own nearly depleted loins. Astonishingly, he felt himself building swiftly to a climax. He grabbed her thighs and began pulling her down brutally onto his erection and in a few wild, explosive moments, it was all over.

And this time he did sleep—until, in order to observe the proprieties, Melanie awakened him with kisses about his face and neck, then helped him dress, after which she pushed him unceremoniously out into the early, predawn darkness.

— Chapter Two —

Joe Meek nudged Hawk awake the next morning and told him that Hank Shaw, the train's captain, wanted them both. Now.

"What's up?" Hawk asked, flinging aside his blanket.

"Blackfoot."

Shaw was waiting for them by the lead wagon. A few anxious settlers were with him. Someone thrust a steaming cup of coffee into Hawk's hands. He took it gratefully and began to sip.

Hank Shaw was not the same captain the members of the wagon train had elected when they left Wisconsin territory. From all accounts, the first one had proven spectacularly inept, managing to lose three wagons while crossing the Red River of the North. His incompetence had been enough to send him packing, at which time Shaw had been elected to lead the wagon train the rest of the way. From what Hawk had seen these past two weeks, it had been a good choice.

In the Bible Hawk kept back at his cabin in the

mountains above the Snake, there were drawings of
Old Testament prophets. Hawk thought Shaw bore
a startling resemblance to them. Six feet tall with a
solid, square block of a face, he had dark, handsome
eyes that peered out from under a granite brow.
The lower portion of his face was covered with a
dark, well-trimmed beard. He favored dark trousers
and shirts and wore a black floppy, wide-brimmed
hat. At the moment he was puffing reflectively on
his clay pipe, while the others sipped hot coffee
and tried to keep warm in the early morning chill.

When he saw Hawk and Joe Meek had been given
a cup of coffee, he took the clay pipe out of his
mouth and turned to one of the settlers, Thurston
Welby.

"You tell 'em, Welby."

A blond rake-handle of a man, Thurston Welby
shifted his feet and ran long fingers through his
thinning hair. "Last night my milch cow must've
wandered away from the wagons looking for fresh
grass. Well, I just found her. She was all butchered
up not far from the train."

"Indians," snapped Shaw.

Joe Meek spat a glob of tobacco juice. "Blackfoot,
more'n likely."

"Welby's milch cow ain't all they got," Shaw
added. "I had someone check the cavvy. They took
four horses. One of them was my blue."

"And two of my oxen," a settler in the rear piped
up, pushing through the growing circle of anxious
settlers, his long, rawboned face grim.

"They're tryin' to bleed us to death," Welby complained. "We're like Christmas trees to them red

devils. They'll strip us clean by the time we reach the mountains."

Shaw fixed Joe Meek with his dark eyes. "Well, Joe," he said. "What's your advice?"

Joe shrugged. "You want Hawk and me to run off the Blackfoot Nation. Is that it?"

"I want your advice, dammit! You're supposed to know all about these aborigines. Tell me how I should deal with them. Perhaps some trade goods. A few horses. But we must avoid bloodshed at all costs."

"You don't want bloodshed," Joe Meek repeated.

"You heard me."

Cocking his head, Joe Meek looked at Hawk. "You want me to tell him?"

"Go ahead."

Joe Meek turned back to Shaw. "The pure and simple truth is you got no business taking these pilgrims through Blackfoot country, Shaw," Joe Meek told the captain bluntly. "And the only way to deal with the Blackfoot is go south through Crow country. These northern plains belong to the Blackfoot, and you jaspers ain't welcome. In the past ten years Blackfoot warriors have scalped and otherwise disposed of more than two hundred trappers—along with a neat assortment of pilgrims and other poor fools. I already told you this when you hired me on and that's why I asked Jed to come with us and help scout."

"You mean you're telling us to go through South Pass—to abandon our present itinerary."

"You said you wanted to avoid bloodshed. That's the only sure way to do that."

"But that would mean traveling twice the distance—and when we get through South Pass, we'll likely end up losing half our wagons and stock trying to get down the Columbia. One party I was with in thirty four lost half its wagons and most of its stock tryin' to navigate that river through the gorge."

Joe expectorated a black streak of chewing tobacco. "This child is sure sorry to hear about that, Captain," he said, "but I ain't the one told you to make this trip to Oregon. You asked for advice. I'm givin' it. Now the Blackfoot know we're here, I say go south—if you want to reach Oregon with all your hair, that is."

An angry mutter swept through the growing throng of settlers. Hawk understood the reasons for their reaction perfectly. They had been on this trek long enough. They wanted to end it—and soon. Ahead of them in the distance, clearly visible now for close to a week, rose the dim ramparts of the Rockies. Beyond that last barrier, they knew, was Oregon. It was so close they could already smell the apple blossoms on the trees they would plant. As far as they could see, they were nearly to the Promised Land. Turning away now was unthinkable.

"No," Shaw said decisively, reading correctly the faces of every settler there. "We're not turning tail and running south. We're going on. When I hired you on, Joe, I told you there'd be a party from Fort Walla Walla coming up the Clearwater to meet us when we get through the mountains. Well, we're going to be there to meet them."

Hawk spoke up then. "From what Joe told me, you folks still have to find a way through them mountains."

"Joe has assured us we can. And if he's no longer willing to help us find it, we'll find it ourselves."

"Don't worry none about that," the mountain man assured Shaw. "I said I would help you through the mountains, and I will. But a minute ago, you just asked me what to do about them Blackfoot, and I told you."

"And you have my answer."

"You mentioned something about dealing with them."

"Yes. I don't see why we couldn't arrange something. All we want is for them to let us pass through their country in peace."

Joe Meek turned to Hawk. "What about it, Jed? Think we can manage that?"

"I'll ride out this morning," Hawk told Joe, "and see if I can overtake those Blackfoot who took our goods last night. Maybe we can work something out. But I doubt it."

"Do your best then."

Hawk nodded.

"Want me to come along?"

Hawk shook his head. "No need for that. You got a pass to find. Remember?"

An hour later, most of the gear he would need on his pack horse, Hawk rode back to Melanie Fitzpatrick's wagon to look in on Melanie and see how Tommy was doing. Pulling his mount to a halt beside the wagon, he leaned his head in. Tommy was with his mother, sitting up and looking as chipper as a woodpecker in springtime as Melanie fed him porridge from a bowl.

"Hi, Tommy," Hawk said. "You feelin' any better?"

"Sure," he said, his voice a little hoarse, "but I got a headache from all that whiskey."

"That won't last long. I know from experience."

"That's what I told him," Melanie said, glancing at Hawk almost shyly, "but I wasn't relying on any personal experience."

"I'm ridin' out," Hawk told her. "Keep close to the wagons from now on. We got visitors."

"I heard. Blackfoot."

He nodded, then looked back at Tommy. "You keep that rifle handy, Tommy. Your ma'll be countin' on you."

"I sure will, Mr. Hawk."

With a quick wave, Hawk wheeled his horse and rode out at a brisk trot, his packhorse barely able to keep up. He didn't figure finding the Blackfoot would be any problem. They had left plenty of sign for him to follow, including—not far from the wagon train—the mangled, mutilated carcass of Thurston Welby's milch cow. A mile farther on he found the two oxen butchered clumsily, one whole side missing.

He'd find them—if they didn't find him first.

When he caught up to them in a wooded valley a little after sundown the next day, he found they weren't Blackfoot, after all—but allies of the Blackfoot, Gros Ventres. And there were only three of them, which explained why they had been careful to work as stealthily as they had.

Now, a day later and figuring they were far enough

away from the wagon train to celebrate their great victory, the Big Bellies had built a roaring bonfire and were sitting cross-legged around it, feasting on the oxen and relating boastfully to each other their awesome courage and bravery. Plundering a sleeping wagon train had done great things for their morale and would do even greater things for their reputations.

Looking about the camp site, Hawk saw they had taken more than the settlers had realized. Not only was Shaw's blue in evidence, but six other fine eastern saddle horses had been taken as well. In addition, clothing, cooking utensils, sacks of salt and flour—and even some of the buffalo meat set aside for jerking—had been carried off.

They weren't eating that, however.

They were devouring the side of oxen they had carried with them from the wagon train, and as was customary with these gluttons, they had been unable to wait until the beef had been cooked through thoroughly and were now devouring it half cooked, the blood flowing freely down their faces, elbows, and over their swollen bellies. Then Hawk saw the barrel of apple jack that had been roped to the side of one of the wagons. It was now doing a fine job standing in for trader's whiskey.

Hawk moved back into the shadows to wait.

Sodden with meat and drink, the three Gros Ventres slept where they had eaten without posting a sentry. When Hawk walked silently over to their sprawled forms, he gazed down at them with a fine contempt. They were dead to the world. The still-bright coals of their bonfire lit clearly their slack faces and bloated bellies. If Hawk had been of such a mind, he could have bent over and calmly driven his bowie into each one of them.

Instead, he bound the warriors' ankles together with his reata. So swiftly and gently did he work that only one of them came awake, and when he did, Hawk clubbed him back to sleep with the barrel of his revolver. Next, he tied all three warriors' hands behind them. By that time all three were fully awake, twisting wildly and spitting at him like caged wildcats.

Grinning, he went back for his mount and packhorse. After loading up the packhorse with as much of the loot as it could carry back, Hawk rounded up the wagon's stolen horseflesh along with those ponies belonging to the three Gros Ventres. Then he dallied his reata around his saddle horn and, more in fun than anger, dragged the three cursing warriors through their bonfire's embers, thoroughly scorching their backsides.

Some distance from the campsite, Hawk cut the Indians loose. A plains Indian afoot is a pathetic sight, and out of pity for the three inept warriors, Hawk waited until he reached the horizon then set loose their ponies to spare the three warriors the terrible humiliation of having to walk back into their village. Then, driving the wagon train's stolen horses before him, he set out to catch up to the wagon train.

The three ponies belonging to the Gros Ventre warriors did not return to their owners, however.

Instead, they drifted westward and later the next day descended into a long wooded canyon and there joined a horse herd belonging to a band of Blood Blackfoot, the Red Legs. The next morning the ponies were discovered. From their markings it was clear they belonged to the Blood's Gros Ventre allies.

Not long after, Black Feather left the village and rode out of the canyon with a small body of warriors to investigate the matter. They had not ridden far when they caught sight of the three Gros Ventre warriors, foot-sore and weary, toiling over the prairie toward them. Not bothering to mask his contempt, Black Feather rode up to them and slipped from his pony.

"Black Feather of the Red Leg band welcomes his Gros Ventre brothers," he told them, not bothering to mask his disdain for their predicament.

All talking at once, the three warriors hastened to explain what had happened. Glancing amusedly at his fellow tribesmen, Black Feather held up his hand to halt the torrent of explanations.

"Enough," he told them. "Your ponies are waiting in our village. They are fed now and well watered. Ride back with us and say no more to any in our village. Later, in our council, we will hear your story."

At once the Gros Ventres realized the wisdom of Black Feather's words. If their disgrace was known to the women and children of this band, the three warriors would have no peace while they stayed here—or anywhere else in the Blackfoot Nation, for that matter. Without protest, they sat up behind their hosts and rode with them back to the village.

They were still subdued when they told their story that night in the privacy of the council tent. Courtesy prevented the chiefs present from laughing outwardly or showing any mirth at their allies' disgrace at the hands of the lone settler who had so completely surprised them. But it was clear that the Blackfoot chiefs were highly amused, except for a sober few.

One of those not amused was Black Feather. Nearly recovered from the wounds he had suffered at the hands of that mad trapper less than a month before, he leaned forward intently at the conclusion of the Gros Ventres' account and asked them to describe the lone settler who had surprised them and taken back their booty.

The least obese of the three Gros Ventre warriors spoke up. "This white man was tall, even for the white man, and he must have been a chief among the wagon people."

"Why do you say this?"

"His hair was long enough to reach his shoulders."

"And what color was it?" Black Feather asked sharply.

"Gold, like the sun."

Frowning intently, Black Feather demanded, "Was his face like that of a hawk?"

"It was night. I cannot be sure," the warrior said.

But one of his companions, remembering the white man's blade of a nose and his keen blue eyes as he leaned close to tie his ankles, spoke up quickly. "Yes," he told Black Feather. "This man had the face of a hawk."

"You fools! The white man who shamed you was

Golden Hawk! His medicine is great—and he is an enemy to all Blackfoot. Had you been more vigilant, you would have had a great trophy to display to us this day, the scalp of Golden Hawk!"

An uneasy murmur ran through the circle of chiefs. The three warriors were dismissed and as soon as they filed out, Bear Chief stood up and glanced about him, his eyes blazing with defiance.

"Not only have the Big Knives sent a wagon train of settlers to leave their shit and piss on our grass, they have sent Golden Hawk to escort it. As Black Feather says, his medicine is great. But I say it is no greater than that of our warriors. I say this wagon train will not travel across our land unscathed. We must destroy it as a warning to all Big Knives who would cross Blackfoot land. Hear me. This wagon train must be wiped from this earth—and the scalp of every man, woman, and child taken."

Bear Chief's words aroused some, disturbed others. There was a quiet but steady murmur as the chiefs spoke to their neighbors. Then Weasel Tail, always the conciliator, stood up to speak.

"Now hear me, chiefs. Until this day we have spoken only of our need to chastise the miserable Flatheads. They trade now for the white man's weapons and they think it is time to hunt the buffalo on our land. What do we want? To attack this wagon train—or leave Golden Hawk until another time while we teach these Flatheads what it means to challenge the great Blackfoot Nation?"

Before another chief could reply, Black Feather stood up. Though he was one of the youngest of their chiefs, the council members knew him as a courageous and deadly warrior. Already his body bore the scars of his many personal combats, and he had accomplished many coups.

"Hear me, great and venerable chiefs," Black Feather said in a voice the older chiefs found melodious and pleasing. "There is no need for us to quarrel. I too say it would be wise for us to move into the land of the Flatheads and chastise properly these contemptible people for their continued insolence." He paused a moment, then continued. "But the Gros Ventres tell us the wagon train is heading for the mountains. And once these wagon people reach that broken land, they will have deep ravines and narrow passes to negotiate, swift rivers to cross. It is then that we, finished with the contemptible Flatheads, will feed on these wagon people as the terrible night owl feeds on the mice that flee through the grass."

Black Feather sat down.

The discussion was heated at times, but it did not last long. A vote was taken and Black Feather's compromise—to punish the Flatheads first, then attack the wagon train—was accepted. But before the chiefs left, Bear Chief stood up to ask one final question of Black Feather.

"Tell me, Black Feather—what do we do about Golden Hawk?"

"Leave him to me."

Satisfied, the members of the council filed from the council lodge.

—— Chapter Three ——

The settlers saw Hawk coming. Word passed quickly down the wagon train, and before Hawk reached it, Shaw had halted the wagons and with a few others rode out to meet him. Hawk was still driving before him the saddle horses he had taken back from the Gros Ventres, and as Shaw reined in beside Hawk, his eyes gleamed with pleasure at the sight of his prized blue milling about with the other saddle horses.

"You're back soon, Jed!" he cried. "Does this mean you've done it? Do we have a truce with the Blackfoot?"

"We have nothin' of the sort," Hawk drawled. "There weren't any Blackfoot to begin with—just three Gros Ventres on a sneak raid."

"Gros Ventres?"

"You heard me."

"You sure of that?"

Hawk looked at Shaw, his eyes cold. He didn't like men to question what he told them. "You callin' me a liar, Shaw?"

"Hell, Jed. You know better than that. But aren't the Gros Ventres Blackfoot allies?"

"They are. But from the look of it, these three acted on their own. I surprised them and took back what I could."

"Then we have nothing to fear from the Blackfoot?"

"I didn't say that. All I'm saying is that it wasn't a Blackfoot war party that ran off these horses and robbed the wagon train."

But this was enough for the settlers now crowding around. Overjoyed, the men slapped each other's backs, some shouted, others did an impromptu jig. Hawk let the settlers take the packhorse and its retrieved goods back to the wagon train, while he continued on to the train.

He was not as sure as the settlers were that they had nothing more to worry about from the Blackfoot, but he realized how fruitless it would be for him to try and puncture the settlers' balloon. They lived on hope—sometimes when hope could not be justified. But Joe Meek had already warned them and they had chosen not to listen.

And that was that.

A week later, on his way back from the mountains, Joe Meek met the wagon train. A freshly killed buck antelope was draped over his cantle, and he had good news for Shaw. He had found a broad canyon leading through the first mountain range. And in the foothills just ahead of them, he reported not only plenty of fresh water and forage for the stock, but an abundance of wild game. As this news swept along the wagon train, the spirits of every settler soared, and in the days that followed, the wagon train made excellent time, accomplishing distances of twelve, fifteen, and sometimes even twenty miles a day.

Yet the mountains still loomed on the horizon before them, seemingly not a mile closer. Many wondered openly if that great, massive rampart was only a mirage until—as suddenly as a sunrise—the ground lifted under their groaning wagons, their oxen began to labor, and they found themselves in higher, rolling country, the distant mountain flanks suddenly close upon them, their furrowed slopes and pine-studded crags standing out clearly against the sky.

As the wagon train kept on, parties of armed settlers left it to hunt fresh game and found all they could shoot, bringing down antelope, deer, and even a lone buffalo cow one group managed to drive into a small ravine. In the nights that followed, the smell of roasting venison and buffalo filled the air and the swift, high-stepping call of the fiddle sang out as settlers danced in celebration of the completion of their long trek across the northern plains.

As the wagon train approached the canyon passage Joe Meek had found, he and Hawk entered the canyon and scouted ahead. As Joe Meek had already discovered, there was plenty of room for the wagons, and throughout the canyon's length, they found its slopes heavily wooded, a broad stream meandering through the center of it. Beyond the valley, however, they found only a barren upland plain, further progress blocked by yet another mountain range, this one still higher than the first, with more snow-tipped peaks looming behind it, the towering crags resembling titanic picket fences lined up one behind the other, each barrier calling for difficult, if not impossible, exertions from the settlers if they were to get through with their goods and their wagons intact.

Not to mention their lives.

Both men realized what this meant for the members of the wagon train, and when they returned to it, they discussed with Shaw the reality of what lay ahead. But when they finished, Shaw simply puffed on his clay pipe for a moment, then told Joe Meek and Hawk that he was certain they would find a way through the mountains still ahead and cautioned Hawk and Joe Meek. Then he asked them not to pass on to the rest of the settlers what they had just told him.

"Why not?" Hawk asked.

"I don't want to alarm them," Shaw replied. "The women especially."

"It's a little late for that, isn't it?"

The three men were speaking softly around a fire near Shaw's wagon. Shaw, Hawk had noted from the beginning, had been careful to keep his voice down as they conversed.

"Maybe it is, Jed. But that's what I want. Look, everyone in this wagon train is committed to this passage to Oregon. There's no going back now. And I see no point in dampening the good feeling the settlers have now. This optimism will be needed if what you tell me is true."

"It's true," said Joe Meek shortly.

"Then why puncture their balloons now?"

"You don't think you should warn them? So they can get ready?"

Shaw laughed. "They're as ready as they will ever be. So what's the sense of telling them now something they'll be finding out for themselves later."

"And you don't see nothin' wrong with that, Shaw?" Joe Meek asked.

"Dammit, Joe, it don't matter now what lies ahead. One way or another we'll fight our way through to Oregon. It don't matter the cost."

And that ended the conversation. As Hawk and Joe Meek left the wagon train captain, Hawk could not help brooding on what cruel turns the trail ahead had yet to take. Maybe it didn't matter what the cost, as Shaw insisted, but he couldn't help thinking of what this meant for Melanie and her son Tommy.

In a secluded grove of alders and cottonwood close by the river, Hawk and Melanie pulled apart from each other, panting softly, then lay still for a while in each other's arms.

Though they were well out of sight of the wagons, they were still within hailing distance. Tommy, completely recovered from his injuries by this time, was under Ma and Pa Bounty's care this evening. Winking slyly, Ma Bounty had suggested the arrangement that afternoon.

Melanie sat up and began to comb out her long, auburn hair. She had deliberately not put back on her skirt and blouse and was crouching before Hawk on the blanket, devilishly aware of how much he enjoyed gazing upon her fully endowed body. It was night and her large breasts glowed in the soft moonlight filtering through the leaves. Stirring restlessly, Hawk avoided the gleam in Melanie's eye.

Hawk looked back at the wagons. All during their lovemaking he had been aware of the fiddle's squeak and the twanging of a Jew's harp that came from one of the wagons.

"What is it, Jed?" Melanie asked. "Is something troubling you?"

"Does it show?"

"Not before it didn't." She smiled. "But right now you're frowning."

"Hear that fiddle?"

"Of course."

"There's been a lot of celebrating since we reached this canyon. Seems to me everyone thinks Oregon is sittin' there waiting on the other side."

"Why, Jed! Of course it is. Once we're through the mountains, we'll be on the Clearwater. We'll be in Oregon."

"No, you won't. You'll be facing still more mountains, damned higher mountains than these—and so far, Joe's had no luck finding a way through them."

"But he will, won't he?"

"You mean like he found a way through this mountain."

"Yes."

"Maybe yes, maybe no. No matter what, you and your people still have a long, tough way to go."

Seeing how serious he was, she put on her clothes, then pinned up her hair. "Jed," she asked somberly, "is it really that bad?"

"I don't want to alarm you. But I think it's too damn soon for all this celebrating. No matter what you think, Melanie, you ain't in Oregon yet—and the hardest part of this trek is still ahead."

She took a deep breath. "Jed, do you think I should tell Ma and Jake Bounty, or any of the others?"

"That's up to you. But Shaw doesn't want to alarm anyone." He smiled bleakly. "Besides, there's still a chance Joe will find a way through. He's gone north to look now. The thing is, even if he does find a trail through these mountains, it won't be an easy one—not like this canyon."

As he spoke, Hawk leaned back against the cottonwood. Melanie reclined on the blanket, resting her head in his lap. Smiling down at her, he dropped a hand lightly over her breast and held it there. She closed her hand over his and said nothing more.

After a while he chuckled softly. "Maybe I shouldn't have spouted off like that. No sense borrowing trouble. I guess you'll get through, all right."

"Of course we will, Jed."

"You'll just have to be careful."

"We will." She smiled up at him. "Does all this mean you're concerned about us, are you?"

"Yes."

"Jed, does that mean you'll be staying with us when we reach the Clearwater?"

"I'm afraid not."

"Why, Jed? You know you'd be welcome."

He had expected this question and had told himself that when it came he would answer it honestly, so he did not hold back. "You'll be building homes and farms, won't you, Melanie? You and the others. You'll be giving the towns in Oregon city streets and stores and maybe even a sawmill or two. I've heard the other settlers talking."

"Why, yes, of course we will, Jed. It's a new country just waiting for us. We'll plant orchards and make parks!" Her excitement at the prospect caused her to sit up and face him. "We'll have cattle and horses grazing on our fields. We'll be bringing civilization to a wild land."

"That's just the trouble."

"Trouble? I don't understand."

"I just came back from civilization, Melanie. I was visiting my sister Annabelle in Cambridge," he told her, "near Boston."

"Why, that's all the way back east, in Massachusetts."

"That's where it is, all right. I was invited to spend Christmas with Annabelle and her husband. I missed Christmas and didn't get there until March. Believe me, Melanie, I tried to get used to the smoke and the stench and the smell of too many people with too many clothes on, but I couldn't. I don't think I took a single deep breath all the time I was there. I really do wonder how long my sister can hold out. She loves her husband very much, but if it weren't for that, I'm sure she'd be on her way back out here to this country."

"How long did you stay?"

"I was supposed to stay a month or so. But all I could manage was three weeks."

He went silent then, thinking again of that long journey to the eastern coast of the United States and of his disappointment at reaching there—the appalling crowds, the dirt, the smoke. Everything about it. He contrasted that with how good he felt when he got off the steamboat at Fort Union and met the other mountain men, all of whom seemed so glad to see him.

It was as if, like Lazarus, he had come back from the dead.

And maybe he had, after all.

Melanie laid her head back so that it rested once more in his lap. He gazed down at her and saw an intent frown on her face.

"So you don't want any part of civilization," she told him ruefully. "Is that it?"

"Not if it means leaving these mountains, these plains. I have my own place, a cabin north of Fort Hall, near the Snake River. I'll be on my way back to it as soon as you folks make it through these mountains."

She said nothing for a long while, then she asked softly, "Do you live alone in that cabin, Jed?"

"No."

"Is she an Indian woman?"

"Yes."

"What's her name?"

"Raven Eyes."

After a long silence she said, "I see. It's . . . it's a lovely name. What tribe is she from?"

"Crow."

"And she is very beautiful."

"Yes, she is."

"Where is she now, with you so far away in Cambridge and then coming all this way to scout for us?"

"When I left, she said she'd visit her sister's people. As far as I know, she's still back with them."

"Do you think she would understand about . . . you and me?"

"Yes."

"But she would be hurt."

He shrugged.

"Do you miss her?"

"Yes."

"Very much?"

"I miss her. Let's leave it at that."

"Then you've been lonely for her?"

"Yes."

"Have I . . . helped any, Jed?"

"Of course."

"And you've helped me."

"I'm glad."

She said nothing for a long while, then sighed. "Thank you for telling me about Raven Eyes, Jed. I would have asked sooner, but I could feel something there—and I didn't want to pry."

He leaned down and kissed her on the lips. Responding instantly, she reached up and entwined her arms around his neck, returning his kiss with such passion, he knew that what he had just told her had only served to increase her desire for him.

His hands reached under her blouse for her breasts, and as he squeezed one of them, he felt her nipple grow rigid under his palm.

In a moment they were on the blanket together. They kissed wildly, devouring each other. He swept her buttocks under him and felt her legs open for him. His entrance was swift, his lunge powerful, heedless of her gasp, aware now only of his own need for her.

And while they heaved, sweating, slamming with unashamed lust at each other, Hawk could still hear coming from the wagons the high, strident scratch of that damned fiddle.

A day later, just as the settlers emerged from the pass, Joe Meek returned to the wagon train. The wagons had slowed at news of his approach and it was an anxious group of settlers that crowded around his horse when he brought it to a halt beside Shaw's wagon. Hawk had come in from scouting an hour before, and he was waiting with Shaw to hear what news Joe Meek had brought.

The settlers had by now had a chance to inspect fully the plateau stretching ahead of them, not to mention the formidable wall of mountains beyond. Most of the settlers had already noticed the scarcity of vegetation, while others had fixed their concern on the awesome barrier of snow-tipped peaks now blocking their way.

"Well?" Shaw asked as Joe Meek dismounted.

"Relax," Joe Meek said with a grin. "I found a way through. Now someone give me a cup of coffee."

At once, it seemed, a steaming cup of black coffee was thrust into his hand.

Sipping it, Joe Meek continued his report. "There's a gorge about thirty miles north of here. It cuts clean through the mountains. I explored the son-of-a-bitch as far as I could in the time I had. Looks to me like it goes all the way through. But you'd still be pretty high when you got to the end of it—and it sure won't be easy from there."

A quick, excited murmur swept through the settlers. Joe Meek held up his hand to quiet them.

"I'm warnin' you all," he cried, speaking up so all could hear. "There's a mess of boulders at the head of this gorge, an' the only way around is through the stream bed cuttin' through the gorge."

"We'll get through it, all right," said Shaw. "Never you mind about that!" He turned to the settlers crowding eagerly around, and with a mighty shout, cried, "Wagons turn! We're heading north to Oregon!"

The men raced back to their wagons.

A moment later, watching the wagons creaking into their long, northward turn, Hawk turned to Joe Meek.

"I'd like to see that gorge, Joe."

Joe nodded wearily. "Just let me rest these bones awhile."

They found a campfire still burning and sat around it, Joe Meek still sipping his coffee. Hawk watched the wagons rumble past. When Melanie's wagon creaked by, he waved to her. Tommy was riding alongside, his rifle held proudly across his saddle. As the boy waved to him, an uneasy fore-boding fell over Hawk. Tommy was just so damned eager to use that rifle.

Joe Meek sent a black arrow of tobacco at the fire. He was watching the wagons too. "I tell you what, hoss," he said softly. "I ain't done them pil-grims much of a favor. Wait'll you see that gorge."

Well ahead of the wagon train, Hawk and Joe Meek reached the gorge Joe had discovered. That he had found it at all was a miracle. Hidden behind colossal boulders taller than houses, the gorge was screened from sight by thick stands of beech, alder, and pine. Dismounting, Joe showed Hawk where the settlers would have to cut a trail through the timber to get down to the stream. Once there, the wagons would have to make use of the gravel bed to skirt the boulders and regain the floor of the gorge further on.

Leading their horses, Hawk and Joe Meek cut through the trees to the stream bank. Hawk could see the stream's gravelly bottom through the swift, icy water—as clearly as through a windowpane. It looked solid enough, and if it stayed that way until the wagons got past the boulders, the wagon train would be all right. Mounting up, the men rode through the water until they could come out onto the stream bank.

Splashing up onto the bank, Hawk and Joe Meek dismounted to look around. Hawk glanced up at the steep, towering walls of the gorge. He could see where the stream had cut through layer after layer of solid rock, each one sharply different in texture and color. The trail alongside the stream was narrow, though it looked wide enough to take the wagons through without too much trouble. There was little room for error, however. The steep walls kept out most of the sunlight, while trapping much of the stream's moisture. At best, this would be a dank, clammy trail.

"Further on," Joe Meek told him, "the wagons will have to cross over to the other side. I marked the ford they'll have to take. Shouldn't be much of a problem, but you never know."

"Is that the only problem, Joe?"

"Nope."

"Go on. I'm listening."

"This here gorge empties out onto a mountainside. I didn't dare describe this to Shaw. Beyond this gorge are canyons and mile-deep gullies, a real mess of 'em. Them settlers'll be hauling their wagons a long time before they ever start to use them again. And there's still mountains after that."

Hawk nodded. It was about what he had expected. Anyway, he thought as he looked around him, there was plenty of wood, and there would be an abundance of fresh water.

"How long is this gorge, Joe?"

"About three, maybe four miles. But the walls ain't near this close further on."

"All right. You go on back and bring the wagons up, Joe. I'll scout ahead."

As Joe meek stepped into his saddle, Hawk let his glance travel up the steep, sheer walls. He shaded his eyes to see the rim more clearly. The trees growing on it were so distant they looked as insubstantial as toothpicks.

"Maybe I'd better have a look up there too."

"Good idea," Joe Meek said, turning his mount. "We're still pretty damn close to Blackfoot country."

Hawk watched the little mountain man lead his horse into the stream and splash out of sight around a boulder, then looked back up at the rim. He nodded grimly.

That's just what he had been thinking.

— Chapter Four —

Hawk rode beside the stream for a quarter of a mile before he came upon a break in the canyon wall and followed it up to the rim of the gorge. Riding back along it, he looked for sign of Blackfoot and found none. He felt a little better, but his uneasiness persisted. The gorge below would be a hell of a place for the settlers to be ambushed by a determined Blackfoot band. A force not half their size could wipe out the entire wagon train.

When he reached a spot above the entrance to the gorge, he glanced back the way he had just ridden and saw still higher peaks looming on the western horizon. As Joe Meek had pointed out, even after the settlers made it through this gorge, the trail ahead would offer them only more grief. Hawk shook his head wearily and looked to see if the wagons were in sight. All he could see were the dust clouds they were raising. But they were getting close and should reach the entrance to the gorge by nightfall.

Hawk rode back along the rim, returned to the floor of the gorge, and kept on through it, hoping to spot a trail the wagons might take when they cleared it. Riding northwest, he came to a break in the solid mountain flanks and found himself looking through a wide gap at an unbroken sweep of timber-clad foothills. Peering closer, his eyes caught the distant gleam of a river slicing between one pair of foothills. Hawk was elated. It looked like he might have found a passage through the mountains—one that might just take them all the way to the Clearwater!

Hawk's elation vanished as soon as it came. There was trouble a lot closer than those distant foothills. Three, then four columns of smoke pumped sky-ward to hang like dirty clouds over the nearest stretch of timber. He knew at once what that meant. They had long since crossed into Flathead country, which meant he was witnessing the burning of a Flathead village. Since the Flatheads began arming themselves with rifles and crossing the mountains to hunt buffalo on Blackfoot land, the frequency and savagery of Blackfoot raids on their villages had increased. That meant a Blackfoot war party was in the vicinity.

Hawk leaned back in his saddle and was going to turn his horse when four mounted Blackfoot war-riors materialized on the trail before him. Wheeling completely about, he saw two more Blackfoot cut-ting him off from behind.

Hawk lashed his horse and sent it headlong through the gap, down the rock-strewn slope toward the timber far below, the Blackfoot after him in full cry. His mount almost went down twice during its wild plunge, but Hawk hauled him upright each time, and when he reached the bottom, he turned without slackening speed and rode full-tilt into the timber. A branch whipped at his face, almost knocking off his hat. He ducked low and kept going until he came to a stream. Dismounting swiftly, he snaked his rifle from its scabbard, lashed the horse's rump, and sent it plunging on across the stream into the timber.

Ducking into cover, he watched the Indians charge across the stream after his horse. As soon as they had vanished, he left the brush and ran back through the timber, intending to make it back to the gorge entrance in time to warn the settlers of the Blackfoot war party's presence. He had almost reached the slope down which he had plunged not long before when he heard behind him the pounding of unshod hooves. He spun to see two Blackfoot warriors almost on him. Before he could fling up his rifle to fire, a Flathead Indian leaped out of the brush and swept the closest Blackfoot off his pony.

So close was the nearest warrior, Hawk had no clear shot at him. Reaching up, he grabbed the pony's bridle and twisted the pony's head around with such force it went down on one knee, pitching the Blackfoot over its neck. Before the savage could regain his feet, Hawk buried his bowie, hilt deep, between his shoulder blades.

Withdrawing the knife, he turned to see the Flathead on the ground under the other Blackfoot, who was about to bring down his upraised knife. Hawk snatched up his rifle and swung it like a club, its barrel catching the Blackfoot on the side of his head. The stunned warrior flipped over onto his back. Before Hawk could finish him off, the Flathead leaped up, grabbed the Blackfoot's knife, and plunged it into his chest.

As he stood over the dead warrior, preparing to scalp him, Hawk pulled him into the brush. There was no time for such pleasures. The Flathead understood Hawk's priorities and led him through the timber for at least a quarter of a mile until he reached a bear's den scoured out of a riverbank in under a tangle of tree roots. The Flathead had known of this den and ducked into it, Hawk following in after him. An overpowering bear smell smote Hawk like a fist. He blinked in pure misery and tried not to take any deep breaths. The Flathead crouched across from him, sucking in deep gutfuls of air, as if he were under an apple tree in springtime.

In the Flathead's tongue, Hawk asked the Indian his name.

"From this day I am Two Scalps," the Flathead answered. "And I know who you are. Golden Hawk. Much have I heard of you. But you are like any white man, after all."

Hawk acknowledged this obvious fact with a shrug. "How bad was your village hit?"

"All our lodges are gone. Our old men and women and our children were killed. Our women were taken by the Blackfoot, then killed. Our band is no more."

"It is good you escaped."

"I was bathing in the stream when the Blackfoot devils attacked. I ran back to help, but a Blackfoot knocked me senseless with his war club. When I woke the cries of my people filled the air. I crawled away through the grass and took two Blackfoot scalps before I came upon you." As he spoke he patted two bloody trophies hanging from his belt.

In the den's nearly pitch-dark interior, Hawk could barely make out the Indian's face, except for his strong jawline and his black, gleaming eyes. He was wearing a buckskin shirt, breechclout and leggings, and was at the moment fondling the knife he had taken from the Blackfoot. The knife had a sharp double-edged iron blade, with bear jaws and feathers bound to its bone handle. It was a Blackfoot bear knife, Hawk realized. There were only a few such knives among the Blackfoot tribes, and to own one gave its possessor powerful medicine, for in battle he would be endowed with the unstoppable ferocity of the grizzly.

Hawk reached for it. Two Scalps handed it to him.

"Bear knife is powerful medicine," Two Scalps said. "But medicine did not help much the warrior I took it from. He was cruel warrior. He slew old men and women."

Nodding somberly, Hawk realized the Flathead was thinking of his own ravaged village and the murderous Blackfoot that had stormed through it. He handed the knife back to Two Scalps.

"Will you not also kill old Blackfoot men in return?" Hawk asked. "When your time comes, will you not also ravage their women and kill their children?"

"I hear you. Already this day I have killed three Blackfoot warriors. Two I have scalped and many more scalps will I take. But I think I will be far from the Blackfoot villages when I die, so I do not think I will harm their children or their old men and women."

Hawk did not press the matter.

Suddenly Two Scalps cocked his head, then raised his hand for silence. Hawk heard it too—the steady drum of unshod ponies pounding closer. In a moment the ground over their heads shook as the Blackfoot galloped past. Gradually, the drumbeat of hooves faded.

For some time after, the two remained silent, listening, waiting. Then Hawk glanced out. It was nearly dark now, and since the timber no longer echoed to the sound of pursuit, Hawk figured it was safe for them to get out of the den. Two Scalps agreed. Once outside, Hawk stood up gratefully and sucked in the clean night air. The moon was not up yet, and the trees shut out the night sky.

He turned to Two Scalps. "Golden Hawk thanks Two Scalps. He leaves his friend now to warn his own people. The darkness will protect him."

"Your people, are they in danger from the Blackfoot?"

"I am not sure. Perhaps."

"Then I will go with Golden Hawk. Perhaps we will find more Blackfoot to kill."

Hawk could not argue with that reasoning and the two set off.

Black Feather crouched on a ridge behind a stand of scrub pine that hid him from the gorge below and watched as the wagon train halted.

Without waiting for the next day, the settlers

had hacked all night at the timber that blocked their way to the stream. Then, promptly at dawn, they had driven their wagons through the shallow stream around the boulders and up onto the trail beyond them. Now they were halfway through the gorge and were getting ready to ford the stream to reach a wider trail on the other side.

Black Feather's plan was to launch his attack while the wagons were crossing the stream. Two riders left the wagon train and splashed out into the shallow water, testing the gravelly bottom of the stream bed to make sure it was solid enough for the wagons. Satisfied, the two riders rode up onto the opposite bank and waved the first wagon toward the water. The time for the attack was getting closer, but Black Feather was still waiting to catch sight of Golden Hawk's tall figure.

Someone was approaching from behind. He turned to see Bear Chief step into view. Black Feather was pleased. He had been afraid the fleeing Flatheads had struck Bear Chief down. No matter what his war party might gain in booty and scalps from that Flathead village, the death of a chief as popular as Bear Chief would cast a pall of disaster over the entire raid—and over Black Feather's reputation as well.

"I see many Flathead scalps hanging from your waist," Black Feather told Bear Chief by way of greeting.

"Too many. The filthy Flatheads run like sheep and give a warrior no pleasure in the killing." Then he sobered. "Our warriors are waiting. They grow impatient. The wagons are below us. When do we attack?"

"When I give the signal."

"Why do you wait?"

"I wait for Golden Hawk. When I see him, I will join the warriors and fight my way to his side. His golden scalp will hang from my belt this night."

"You will not take his scalp this night. He is not with the wagons."

"How do you know this?"

"We came upon him while chasing Flatheads. We encircled him, but like the god of lightning he broke past us down a slope and vanished into the timber. We went after him, but his medicine was great. He slew two of our bravest warriors and was gone like smoke in the wind."

Black Feather looked closely at Bear Chief. "You did not see him again?"

Bear Chief shifted uncomfortably before replying. "We searched for him until the moon rose. Then one of us saw his shadow moving after us through the trees high above us. We fled to escape his evil medicine."

A cold shiver ran up Black Feather's back. This Golden Hawk's medicine was indeed great. Black Feather decided to wait no longer. He strode out beyond the screening pine, raised his right hand, then lowered it swiftly, like a blade lopping off an enemy's head.

Thurston Welby was driving the second wagon. As he started into the water after the first one, he snapped his bullwhip repeatedly over the backs of the oxen, anxious that they not slow down and let his wagon wheels get stuck in the gravel. His right hand was still in the air—the snap of his whip sounding like gunshots—when a Blackfoot arrow planted itself in his chest. Without uttering a sound, Welby fell forward into the shallow water and did not move again, nor did he hear the terrified screams coming from his wife in the wagon behind him.

A shot from the canyon wall caused Henry Shaw to turn in his saddle and glance up. A second shot smashed a hole in his face and he tumbled backward off his horse. Behind him, Joe Meek bent low over his mount, kicked it savagely, and cut swiftly toward the brush cover at the base of the canyon wall. Two arrows slammed into his horse's flanks. The animal hurtled to the ground, throwing Joe Meek free. Before the horse began twitching, he was on his feet, running, his rifle in one hand, his bowie in the other. From across the stream behind him, Joe Meek could hear the men and women screaming and the high, bloodcurdling cries of the Blackfoot as they descended on the wagons.

The moment gunfire sounded, Ma and Pa Bounty ducked under their wagon. Ma held a frying pan, Pa was hefting a loaded flintlock rifle he had not fired in anger in all the years he owned it. A Blackfoot warrior caught Ma's hair from behind and dragged her out from under the wagon. Pa turned to deal with him, and an arrow plunged through his back with such force its iron tip protruded from his belly. He looked down at it in horror, then pitched forward. The last sound he heard was Ma, screaming.

*   *   *

In the rear of the next wagon behind the Boun-
tys, Melanie and Tommy crouched, terrified as they
heard Ma's screams suddenly break off. Tommy
held his rifle in readiness, but his knees were weak
and his palms sweaty as sporadic gunfire broke out
all around their wagon. Ahead of him, he saw canvas tops erupting in flames. A flaming arrow whistled past his head and buried itself in a mattress
behind him. He heard his mother scramble back to
beat out the flames.

A Blackfoot warrior loomed up in front of him
and boosted himself swiftly into the wagon. Black
war paint covered his eye sockets and the hollows
of his cheeks and there were broad white streaks
across his forehead. As he raised his huge scalping
knife, there was a triumphant gleam in his eyes.
Behind Tommy, his mother screamed. Reflexively,
Tommy pulled the trigger and saw the Blackfoot's
nose vanish where the round entered. The Blackfoot
flipped backward out of the wagon.

A butcher knife in her hand, Melanie crouched
beside Tommy while he tried with numb fingers to
reload the rifle. He was spilling powder over the
floor of the wagon and could not find wadding and
was about to burst into tears of frustration when a
rifle's blast from the wagon seat behind him punched
a hole in his back, severing his spinal chord. Screaming, Melanie turned to clasp Tommy to her and
received an arrow in her side, then another, both
shafts slamming clear through her to rattle against
the wagon's side. She was still holding on to Tommy
when a Blackfoot's strong hands grabbed her abun-
dant curls and proceeded to scalp her.

*   *   *

The moment Hawk entered the gorge, Two Scalps left him and without a wave vanished into the brush shrouding the base of the wall. The last glimpse Hawk had of him, he was climbing toward the rim.

Hawk continued on, running steadily, his effortless stride devouring the distance, his shock of blond hair flying out from under his broad-brimmed hat. He did not seek cover as he ran, intent only on reaching the settlers before they entered the gorge. He had assumed this would be sometime that morning. But that did not give him much time. Already the sun was high enough to plant a bright band across the top of the gorge. Though his concern regarding the Blackfoot war party might be unfounded, they had not shown him much friendliness the day before, and it was only logical to assume that they might pose a threat to the wagon train.

He kept pounding steadily along, cursing his lack of a horse. Only gradually did he become aware of the brooding silence that hung over the gorge. There was, he realized, no birdsong, nor did he hear the chitter of squirrels or chipmunks in the trees above him. No small animals rustled in the grass to escape his approach. Even the air itself, dank and fetid, was bereft of all movement as it hung between the gorge's high, damp walls.

As he ran, a cold hand closed about his heart. He cocked his head to listen. The silence seemed only to increase. Then, abruptly, he was almost certain he heard the faint popping of gunfire. He pulled up to listen, but all he could hear for sure was the rapid thudding of his heart. Starting up again, he redoubled his pace and kept on until a half mile or so later he swept around a bend in the gorge and came upon the wagon train—or what was left of it.

An involuntary cry of dismay broke from him. Except for one untouched wagon standing in the stream, the settlers' wagons had been sacked, over-turned, and some put to the torch. One of the wagons was still blazing. More ominous still was the silence that now hung over the gorge.

As he ran closer, he saw bodies strewn every-where, some hanging from the wagons, others still on the seats, many with arrows protruding from their chests. The oxen had been bludgeoned and hacked to pieces while still in their traces, and most of the men were mutilated. The women had been staked to the ground, their legs splayed apart, their skirts hiked up over their heads. They did not move as Hawk passed them, their wide eyes staring in fixed horror at the sky.

A muffled sound came from one burnt-out wagon. Hawk approached it quickly, hopefully. Peering in, he saw a Blackfoot warrior kneeling over an old woman, his breechclout untied. He turned at Hawk's approach and lunged at Hawk with his knife. Hawk fired his revolver into the Blackfoot's chest. As the Indian sprawled backward, Hawk climbed hastily past him into the wagon.

The old woman was still alive. Her eyes were closed tightly, her face turned away as she sobbed bitterly, silently, to herself. There were multiple knife wounds in her chest, the blood that issued from them covered by the folds of her dress, which the Blackfoot had flung up over her head. Evidently the Blackfoot warrior had been too preoccupied with his conquest to leave the wagons when his fellows did.

But even as Hawk bent over the old woman, she breathed her last. Hawk backed hastily out of the wagon.

"Watch out, Hawk!"

The warning cry came from across the stream. Hawk turned as a distant rifle cracked. Another Blackfoot—two ponies behind him on a lead—dropped the huge horse pistol he had been aiming at Hawk's back, staggered forward a step, then fell, lifeless, to the ground.

Hawk glanced across the stream. Joe Meek stepped out of cover and waved.

At that moment a high-pitched cry of terror came from the rim above Joe Meek. Glancing up, Hawk saw a Blackfoot warrior tumbling to his death. Two Scalps stepped into view onto the ridge above Joe Meek. As Hawk and Joe Meek waved their thanks, Two Scalps stepped back and vanished.

Leading the two ponies behind him, Hawk went looking for more Blackfoot. But there did not seem to be any. He continued to walk beside the ravaged, burnt-out wagons, his heart aching as he saw how swift and deadly had been the Blackfoot attack. Apparently, not a man, woman, or child remained alive, and of those dead that Hawk recognized, many were scalped and most were mutilated almost beyond recognition.

When he came to Melanie's wagon, he found its

smoldering canvas resting on the frame, the hoops that had held it upright burned completely through. He did not want to look inside, but forced himself and saw Melanie, scalped, still clinging to Tommy, her dress scorched from the flames, her face contorted in death. It was almost too much for him. He turned away, swearing bitterly, deeply, as the memory of the massacre of his family years before welled up inside him.

Joe Meek approached him, his face grim. He had a bandage around his head and another one, dark with blood, around his right thigh. He limped slightly as he approached.

"See you got here, hoss."

"Thanks for that shot, Joe. I owe you."

"You know who that Indian was on the ridge above me? He sure as hell saved my goose, that one."

Hawk nodded wearily. "His name's Two Scalps. He's a Flathead I met. It's a long story. I'll tell you about it later."

Joe Meek nodded and looked gloomily about him. "We better find some shovels. Looks like we got some grisly work ahead of us."

"Joe, I ran into a Blackfoot war party yesterday. I tried to get back here to warn you. But I was afoot."

"Don't go blaming yourself, hoss. This here was comin' at this wagon train the moment it crossed through Blackfoot land. Ain't nothin' either of us could do about that. It's cured me, though."

"Of what?"

"Of guidin' any more wagons west. Let someone else lead these fool pilgrims to slaughter. This child ain't in the business no more."

A distant cry alerted both men. Hawk turned in the direction of the gorge's south ridge from which the cry had come. Then it came again.

"Golden Hawk!"

This time Hawk caught sight of a lone Blackfoot standing on the rim of the gorge. Hawk thought he recognized the Indian—then he remembered. It was Black Feather, the same Blackfoot who was convinced Hawk had been in league with the trapper who had robbed him.

Black Feather waved Hawk closer.

Hawk mounted one of the Blackfoot ponies, left Joe Meek, and rode up the steep slope until he was within a few hundred yards of the Blackfoot. By that time a line of mounted warriors had ridden up to flank Black Feather, their lances at salute, their shields gleaming in the sun.

Black Feather spoke up then, his voice cold. "Come no closer, Golden Hawk. We have lost brave warriors this day, and you sit astride a pony belonging to one of them. There are many in this war party who are as eager as I to bring your scalp back to our village."

"Damn you to hell!" Hawk cried. "Those dead men and women down there should give you and your warriors little pride. This was no battle. It was a slaughter of innocents. These whites were not warriors. All they wanted was to settle in the land beyond these mountains. They did not threaten your buffalo or your fur trade."

"That does not matter. Let this be a warning to all the wagon people who would move through Blackfoot land to cross these mountains. If one wagon train is allowed to pass, others will follow. We know this is true. Warn the wagon people who might be foolish and follow after them. They do not yet own this land. It is Blackfoot land."

He turned to go.

"Do not go yet, Black Feather!" Hawk called. "Remember? We have a score to settle."

"I remember. I told you we would meet again, and we have. Do not worry. There is much time yet. We will settle matters, I promise you. Now I return to my village, so my people will see how much stronger than Golden Hawk's medicine is that of Black Feather."

Pulling his horse back, he vanished from the rim, his mounted warriors following, and a moment later there came the muffled thunder of many hooves. Pushing his pony hard, Hawk rode up onto the rim in time to see the Blackfoot warriors disappearing from sight, driving their stolen Flathead ponies before them.

Black Feather had made his point. Any more settlers who crossed Blackfoot land did so at their own peril. Only the warning had come too late for Melanie and for the other members of the wagon train still smoldering in the gorge below.

Black Feather was right. There would come a time when he and Hawk would settle matters. Hawk would make damn sure of that.

—— Chapter Five ——

Hawk halted his newly acquired pony and looked back down at the gorge—and at the broken wagons and shallow graves they were leaving behind. Beside him, Joe Meek looked back also. Joe Meek was riding Hank Shaw's chestnut, the only saddle horse the Blackfoot had not taken. Hawk was using a dead Indian's pony for a packhorse.

"We better get movin'," Joe Meek remarked. "We done the best we could."

"Trouble is, Joe, them wagons down there won't stop a single settler. All they think of is new towns and fresh ground to rip up with their plows." As Hawk spoke, he looked back down at the graves, singling out the spot where Tommy and Melanie lay together in death's timeless embrace. "It's a kind of crazy fever in them."

"Let's go, hoss," Joe Meek said gently, noting where Hawk's glance was resting. "We can't do any more here."

"Maybe not here. I'm going north."

"After that Blackfoot chief?"

Hawk's grim blue eyes gleamed with resolve as he looked back at Joe Meek. "Maybe you didn't hear him as clear as I did. We've got a score to settle."

"So you're just gonna ride into Blackfoot country and settle it?"

"You know of a better way?"

"I say forget it, Hawk. I know that chief and his Blood band. They're Red Legs, and they're still tough—not growin' soft on white man's whiskey like the Piegans or the Gros Ventres. They ain't never let a trapper yet into their country—and those they find get their head chopped off. Some they cripple permanently as a warning to others."

"I ain't askin' you to come with me, Joe."

"I know that. And I wouldn't, even if you asked me. I'm just tellin' you what I know of them heathens."

"Then I guess we'll be partin' here." Hawk held out his hand.

Joe Meek shook it, then wheeled his horse and set off. Hawk watched him until he reached a rise and turned for a final wave. Hawk returned it, then turned his pony and headed north.

He had taken Henry Shaw's saddle and stored his own Paterson Colt in his saddle bag, replacing it in his belt with a Walker Colt he had found in the wreckage of the wagons. The big Walker reminded Hawk of one he had lost a few years back. His powder horn and shot bag were full, and he had enough percussion caps to last him through a long campaign.

Which was a good thing. He would need plenty of

firepower if he was going to get that Blackfoot son-of-a-bitch. Firepower—and luck.

A week later, as Hawk placed his coffeepot carefully back onto the glowing embers of his campfire, a familiar trapper stepped out of the brush, his Kentucky rifle leveled at him. Leaning back against the tree behind him, Hawk glanced coolly over at the trapper. This was the same fool that Hawk had caught robbing Black Feather's plews. It was clear, however, that he did not yet recognize Hawk.

"Put that cannon away," Hawk told him quietly. "There's plenty coffee for both of us."

The trapper stepped nearer, his eyes narrowing as he peered more closely at Hawk's face. He did not lower the rifle. Again, Hawk noted the wild, unkempt ugliness of the man with his unshaven face, bridgeless nose, and the jagged white scar that ran down one side of his face. The trapper was as painful to look upon as a chewed-up grizzly. He was dressed no better than the last time the two had met, though his stink had gained some in pungency.

The trapper's mad eyes lit up. "Ain't we met somewheres before, mister?" the trapper asked warily.

"You and me's met before, all right. There was a Blackfoot Indian on the ground that time and you were rescuing his plews. I tried to stop you."

Recognition flashed in the trapper's eyes. Their mean glow hardened. "I remember now! You saved that Blackfoot's hide! He was frying in his own campfire, and you pulled him off it!"

"That's a hell of a way for a man to die."

"He wasn't no man. He was a redskin! You're lucky I didn't kill you." He licked his lips and steadied his rifle. "Maybe now's the time for me to finish the job."

Hawk flung the remnants of his coffee into the man's face. The trapper screamed, dropped his rifle, and pawed frantically at his eyes. Hawk picked up the rifle, swung the butt, and slammed the trapper back onto his ass. Then he threw the rifle to one side and aimed his Walker Colt calmly down at the man.

The trapper blinked unhappily up at him. The coffee had done no permanent damage to his eyes.

"You still robbing Indians?" Hawk asked.

"Him or any other Blackfoot I come upon," the trapper said. He licked his lips and immediately warmed to his topic. "Hell! It don't matter much to me which one I rob, just so long as it's a Blackfoot."

"You got something against the Blackfoot?"

The man's smile was unpleasant. His teeth were broken and discolored. As he replied to Hawk, the hectic gleam of madness in his eyes increased. "If I could, hoss, I'd kill every single one of them. It'd be a merciful favor to every white trapper in this fierce land. But for now, why, I'll just rob and kill any Blackfoot that come close enough."

His Walker Colt still trained on the trapper, Hawk reached for the coffeepot, filled a cup sitting on a log, then handed it carefully to the man. The fellow got to his feet, squinted at the steaming coffee for a moment, then shrugged and took it gratefully from Hawk. It was as hot as the rivers of hell, but he gulped it down greedily and held the empty cup out for more.

"Ran out of makin's a week ago," he explained.

Hawk refilled the man's cup, then sat down and leaned back once more against the tree. Sticking his Walker back into his belt, he watched the man carefully. He didn't trust him, but he felt the trapper was no longer an immediate threat.

"Did I smell beans?" the trapper asked, easing himself down onto a log.

"That you did." Hawk threw a sack of beans at him. "Help yourself. There's salt pork behind you in my provision bag," he told him as the trapper reached for the frying pan next to the fire.

Hawk watched the man cook the beans, the sizzle of the pork filling the dusk, its sharp aroma causing his stomach to twitch hungrily.

"You got a horse?" Hawk asked as he reached out with a spoon and helped himself to a portion of the beans and pork frying in the pan.

"Lost my horse and packhorse."

"Indians?"

The man nodded.

"Blackfoot?"

"No. Gros Ventres."

"Too bad."

"That's all right. I found which way their village was. It ain't far from here. I was on my way to get my horses back when I smelled your coffee."

"How far would you say they were?"

The trapper shoveled a forkful of beans into his mouth. "A day's ride, maybe. These here beans sure taste good. I was sick of rabbit stew and ground squirrels."

Hawk lifted the Walker from his belt to check its load. He had no idea he was that close to hostile Indians and didn't know if he likes having this trapper with him. On the other hand, it might be useful to have a white man as crazy as this one who apparently did not find it impossible to survive in Blackfoot country.

Hawk loaned his packhorse to the trapper and fashioned a makeshift saddle for him, and before dawn they set out for the Gros Ventre village.

The trapper's name was Elias Hogwood.

His history, as he related it to Hawk that morning, was an appalling one, his animosity toward the Blackfoot Confederation the result of an encounter with a Blood war party he had encountered five years before. The Blackfoot had captured him and his four companions, and after taking them to their village, they had slowly roasted Hogwood's fellow captives to death. Being exquisitely skilled in this form of amusement, the Blackfoot women had been able to keep most of the roasting men alive and thoroughly basted for close to three days.

Hogwood had escaped only because a particular species of torture visited upon him by an old chief's young wife aroused in him a fury so wild and uncontrolled that he had broken loose and fallen upon the Blackfoot chief. Slicing off the chief's head with his own steel war hatchet, Hogwood had torn one of the chief's arms from its socket and, using the bloody limb as a war club, had hacked his way through the circle of tormentors. His towering rage and evident madness had been so terrible to witness that all the Blackfoot fell back before him in sheer terror. Then, considering his medicine too powerful to challenge, they had allowed him to flee their village, too shaken to offer any pursuit.

Since that time Hogwood had been a scourge to the Blackfoot Nation. Driven by one single obsession—to find and kill as many Blackfoot men, women, and children as he could—he had continued to trap in their rivers and streams in a bold and direct challenge to every Blackfoot tribe.

This grisly tale Hogwood had related to Hawk in a deep mutter punctuated every so often by an odd clicking sound that came from deep in his throat. What was unsettling to Hawk was not so much the story itself but the relish with which Hogwood told it. That, and his description of the number and variety of Blackfoot scalps he boasted of taking since. The terrible, refined duress of Blackfoot torture had evidently left Hogwood a madman, and an implacable engine of mayhem and murder that fell upon the Blackfoot spring, summer, and winter— like a thunderbolt out of a clear sky.

Now, as they rode through the bright morning, Hogwood glanced slyly over at Hawk and asked him who he was and what in hell he was doing in Blackfoot territory. Hawk gave his name as Jed Thompson and revealed only that he was now after that same Blackfoot he had pulled from the campfire so many weeks before.

"Well, now, ain't that a coincidence." Hogwood

chuckled. "Serves you right for meddlin' in the first place." His mad eyes lit in appreciation of the irony of it. "You should've let that bastard fry."

Hawk knew the trapper was eager to learn why Hawk was now so anxious to get Black Feather, but he did not see any reason for telling him. So he said nothing more on the matter.

A little farther on, Hogwood prodded, "Why didn't you stay back east? Too damn crowded, was it?"

"Crowded and dirty. I'll be glad to get back to the Snake."

"You got a place there?"

"Yep. A cabin—and a Crow woman who I hope will be waitin'."

"Like her, do ye?"

Hawk glanced full at Hogwood. "Yes, I do."

"No need to get your dander up. Just asked. I ain't got nothin' against the Crow. What's she called?"

"Raven Eyes."

He reflected on that awhile, then spoke up. "Had me a woman called Teal Eye once. The damnedest, wildest female I ever did see. Kept her awhile, 'cause she was so damn good on a blanket. But I had to get rid of her finally. Couldn't abide her."

"Why not?"

"She was filthy! Never met a woman so dirty in all my life. I can't abide unclean women."

Hawk found it difficult to believe what Hogwood had just said. And when he thought about it further, he became truly appalled. How dirty must that woman have been to make *this* filthy trapper complain? Hell, even now as they rode through the bright morning, Hawk was doing all he could to keep downwind of Hogwood, so overpowering was the man's stench.

Toward dusk, Hogwood held up his hand. Glancing at Hawk, he grinned, then dismounted, as did Hawk. There appeared to be nothing before them but unbroken prairie, but Hawk knew better. Hidden by this seemingly unbroken series of swales, were deep canyons and long valleys, sliced out of the ground by rivers and streams. As the two led their horses over the next swale, a deep cut in the prairie appeared before them. A moment later, Hawk and Hogwood were peering down at a broad, spacious canyon, its steep sides dropping with precipitous suddenness to the wooded slopes below. A broad, sluggish stream cut through the canyon, along both sides of which sat the Gros Ventre lodges, their teepees extending back into the canyon as far as the eye could see.

The two men mounted up and rode along the rim until the Gros Ventres horse herds came into view. They were grazing at a lush pocket of grassland deep in the canyon. The band had posted no pickets on the canyon rim, obviously feeling quite secure in this valley, hidden away deep in Blackfoot country.

Hogwood rode back along the rim slowly as he peered down intently at the Gros Ventre lodges. Abruptly, he pulled his mount to a halt and pointed.

"There!" he cried, his eyes bright with triumph. "See that lodge near them birches? That's my horse tethered in front of it, and in back is my packhorse. I'll just go down there tonight and take them both back." He glanced sharply at Hawk. "You willin' to help?"

Hawk had business elsewhere, and Hogwood knew this. But Hawk did not see how he could refuse to help this trapper get back his own horseflesh—even if the sonofabitch *was* crazy.

"What's your plan?" Hawk asked him.

"Nothin' to it. We'll just slip down there tonight and raise hell." Hogwood grinned. "You stampede the ponies down through the village. That'll stir them up some—send them runnin' like wet hornets. When the dust clears, I'll be gone with my horses—and anything else I can find."

Hawk realized it sounded simple enough to work.

They made camp near a spring a half mile back of the canyon. They didn't light a fire and Hawk shared what dry jerky he had left with Hogwood. Hogwood's insistent questions forced Hawk to tell him of the Blackfoot wagon train massacre, and his determination to settle the score with Black Feather.

Hogwood laughed, the clicking sound in his throat grating on Hawk. "I tell you what, hoss. If I get that Blood's scalp first, I'll make a trade with you."

"For what?"

"That big Walker you got."

"You're on."

Hogwood chuckled meanly. " 'Course, I might just want to fry him and eat him first. Finish what I started the first time." As Hogwood spoke, tiny flecks of spittle appeared in one corner of his mouth, as if he were salivating in anticipation of just such a meal.

Hawk shuddered and leaned back into the deepening darkness. Sitting this close to pure madness sent an icy shiver up his spine.

They were in luck. The night sky was overcast. The inside of the canyon was as black as the inside of a whore's pocketbook. Hawk left his pony and crept closer to the Gros Ventre brave guarding the band's ponies. Only at the last minute did the Indian hear anything. As he spun around to face Hawk, his eyes wide in surprise, Hawk brought around the barrel of his Walker and smashed the Indian on the side of his face. The sound the steel barrel made crunching into the Indian's jaw was not pleasant. The Indian crumpled to the ground without a cry and Hawk went back for his pony.

Mounting up, he fired his big Colt into the air over the pony's heads. As if they were one single, terrified beast, the ponies stampeded through the moonless darkness down the valley toward the Indian village. Hawk kept after them and soon glimpsed the Gros Ventre village ahead of him. To his surprise it was lit up like a town. Bonfires were everywhere, and the entire population, it seemed, was waiting for him and the stampeding herd. As the ponies charged toward the tepees, mounted Gros Ventre warriors swept out from behind them, swiftly turned their horses, and drove them into the stream, the water effectively slowing them.

It was a trap.

Hawk wheeled his pony in an effort to get away from the mounted braves closing in on him. But out of the darkness whistled a rawhide rope. He felt its heavy strands burning past his cheeks, then coming to rest snugly around his neck. Dropping his reins, he managed to get the fingers of both hands between it and his throat. A split second later he was lifted from his saddle, his heels dragging across the cantle. For an instant he was airborne; then his back hammered into the ground. When his head struck, lights exploded deep inside his skull. For a few dim moments he knew little beyond the fact that he was being dragged rapidly across the damp, grass-covered ground. Then he was being dragged through a fire, the flames beating momentarily against his back like tongues out of hell. He was pulled through at least four more fires and, at the end of it, his buckskins were smoldering like damp firewood. Laughing, the Indians closed about him to stare down at their captive.

Glancing up, Hawk found himself looking at one of the three Gros Ventre warriors he had punished when he had retrieved the horses and other goods they had stolen from the wagon train.

He pushed himself upright and reached for his Walker, intending to sell his life as dearly as possible. But it had fallen from his belt. A crushing blow from behind caught him on the crown of his head and drove him to his knees. As he turned foggily to see who had struck him, a hard-driven boot caught him just in under the ribs, the boot's toe digging in so deep Hawk was sent writhing to the ground.

Only then, flat on his back and gasping for air, did Hawk see that his attacker was Elias Hogwood. Grinning, Hogwood bent over him and waggled in his face the Walker Colt he must have picked up off the ground. Then he reached over and pulled Hawk's bowie from its sheath.

"Thought I didn't know who you was!" he crowed. "Hell! I knew all along you was Golden Hawk! And now I done delivered you to the allies of your Blackfoot enemies."

"You're no better than these savages."

"Never said I was, hoss. I just figured these here no-account Big Bellies would be willin' to bargain for the famed Golden Hawk." He grinned wolfishly. "And I was right. I got my animals back, some furs, and your firearms and gear—and what they get is the mighty Golden Hawk to trade to the Blackfoot." He sobered then, his eyes growing bright with hate. "I'm only payin' you back, you sneaking bastard, for interferin' when I'm about my business."

He straightened up and spat on Hawk.

"You son of a bitch," growled Hawk.

"That's right." Hogwood grinned. "I sure as hell am that."

Still grinning, Hogwood stepped closer and kicked Hawk on the side of his head. Hawk's vision went crimson. He heard wild laughter and the sharp digs of more feet. But that didn't matter as the sound of laughter faded and he tumbled into oblivion.

── Chapter Six ──

Hawk regained consciousness inside a tepee, his wrists and ankles bound tightly with rawhide. Someone was holding a tin cup of water to his lips. As he gulped the water down gratefully, he looked past the cup to his benefactor, and saw the dark, pleasing face of a young Flathead woman bent down close to him, her large, liquid eyes filled with compassion. Once he had drunk his fill, he sat up, pulled his bound legs close, and leaned his back against the lodge poles.

"Who are you?" he asked in the Flathead tongue.

"I am called Walks-in-Water Woman. When the Blackfoot devils kill everyone in my village, I hide in deep water. Only my head is showing when they find me. They sell me to Deer Stalker, chief of these Big Bellies."

"Is this his lodge?"

"Yes. I am his second wife. He does not need two wives. It is only his pride that makes him keep me. He is too old to call me to his couch at night."

"That's too bad."

"For him, yes," she said, her eyes gleaming. Abruptly, she looked about to see that no one was entering the lodge, then leaned close to him and whispered, "He has sent his son to the Blackfoot village. In exchange for you he will gain many fine ponies and blankets. He say the Blackfoot devils have long wanted your golden hair to hang from their scalp poles during their sun dance."

"That's nice to know."

She stood back to take Hawk in, her eyes shrewd. "You are very famous," she told him. "My own people fear you. It is said that at night you fly like the Great Cannibal Owl and eat the hearts of your victims while they are still beating."

"That'd be some trick if I could manage it. What do *you* think, Walks-in-Water Woman?"

"I think you are a man like any other," she said, a sly smile lighting her dusky face. "And maybe more of a man than this old chief."

"You got a good hold on the truth there." He smiled. "Hang on to it."

"Call me Wild Flower. This is what my own people call me before the Blackfoot destroy my village."

Bound as he was, Hawk was unable to reach back behind his neck to see if his throwing knife was still in its sheath. "There's a sheath at the back of my neck," he told Wild Flower. "There should be a knife—see if it is there."

She reached behind Hawk's neck. He felt her light, warm fingers examining the doeskin sheath. "You have a sheath there," she told him. "But there is no knife in it."

Hawk glanced around the tepee until he caught sight of his small, daggerlike throwing knife hanging from a rawhide loop. It was nearly out of sight behind a full quiver of arrows. It looked as if it had been given an honored place among the chief's war paraphernalia.

"All right. I see it now. The knife is hanging over there." He indicated it with a nod of his head. "Can you get it for me?"

She glanced over at the knife, then quickly back at him. "It now belongs to Deer Stalker," she told him in a frightened whisper. "I think he is very proud of this trophy. I dare not take it from him."

At that moment Deer Stalker, followed by his old wife, entered. Wild Flower got to her feet quickly and vanished through the lodge entrance. Ignoring her, the chief strode over to Hawk as his wife dumped a pile of brushwood beside the hearth, then vanished back out for more. The chief gazed down at Hawk for a long moment, his impassive face showing little emotion, though he could not veil entirely the glow of satisfaction in his black eyes.

"Tell me," he said. "Why does the great Golden Hawk not fly from this poor chief's lodge?"

"Wait'll I get my strength back."

The old warrior's flat face creased into a broad smile. He plucked his pipe from a rawhide loop over his couch and lit it carefully, as if he were completely alone in the place. Once he got the tobacco drawing to his satisfaction, he sat down on his couch beside Hawk and handed him the pipe. Hawk's bound wrists caused him some difficulty, but he managed to poke the long stem into his mouth, inhale deeply, and expel the smoke through his lungs. The strong Hudson's Bay tobacco cleared his head. After a few more puffs, he leaned forward and allowed the chief to take his pipe back.

"It is as I thought," the chief said. "Golden Hawk has no wings—only bright hair and a fierce reputation."

"I won't argue with that, chief."

"Many say I should take your scalp before I give you to the Blackfoot. They say it will bring me great honor."

"You'd be trading damaged goods."

The chief nodded in sardonic agreement, then puffed reflectively on his pipe for a while before he spoke again. "The scalps of great warriors this chief does not take often," he told Hawk. "It is bad medicine to take such scalps. This old chief will let his Blackfoot allies have the pleasure of taking your scalp."

"That's real decent of you, chief."

Deer Stalker shrugged "Deer Stalker is a generous chief. All who know him say this. Besides, this old chief has already taken many scalps—most from white trappers."

"You don't like white trappers?"

The old chief's face went cold. "White trappers stink like old fish and come here only to take the wealth from our land and streams. After them will come the forts and then the filthy, stinking towns filled with dirty whites. When I was only a young brave and had no knowledge of the world beyond this place, I journeyed down the Missouri and saw many such towns. In these places the whites live in wooden lodges with heavy roofs that do not open to the sky. Behind these wooden lodges are smaller lodges, and there the white man goes to leave his shit and piss. The stench of such places fills the air in these towns, and yet the whites do not move away but stay on in that stinking place. And each year a new town like it is built closer to the Indian's land." The chief puffed unhappily on his pipe and contemplated this growing menace. Then he sighed and squared his shoulders. "But we will hold them back."

"For how long, chief?"

"As long as we can."

"And how long do you think that will be?"

"Not too long," Stalking Deer admitted wearily. "The whiskey is a great problem. And many of our Blackfoot allies die of the blanket sickness. But this band listens to Stalking Deer's counsel and does not trade at the Big Knives' trading posts and will not accept their sick blankets. We will survive, but not forever, I think."

"Nothing survives forever, chief. Not even the hills and streams. Not even the buffalo."

"Do you think so?"

"Yes. I have heard talk of this in the trading posts. They say the Blackfoot people take too many buffalo hides to trade with the white man at Fort Union."

"It is true," the chief admitted sadly. "The buffalo grow scarce and no longer feed as far north as they once did. Our Blackfoot brothers must now come south to hunt them."

The chief leaned back and went silent then, puffing on his pipe, his eyes looking past Hawk, apparently trying to visualize a time without the buffalo, when no herds at all roamed the high plains. At last he got to his feet and knocked the tobacco from the bowl of his pipe and hung the pipe back on its thong. Then he peered down at Hawk.

"As long as the grass blows in the wind and the sun rises, the buffalo will feed on this land. It has always been so. I will talk to our Blackfoot brothers. Maybe they will take fewer hides."

"I'm not so sure that'll help, chief."

The chief looked warily at Hawk. "Why does Golden Hawk say this?"

Hawk smiled. "I have seen great canyons open in the earth. At the bottom of these canyons is a place the white man calls hell. I warn you, chief. If you challenge the white man's medicine, the herds will disappear into those canyons. Forever."

"And does Golden Hawk have such medicine?"

Hawk shrugged. "It is possible."

The Indian appeared shaken. But he was still capable of bluffing. He said angrily, "Like all white men, you lie."

"I am not like all white men. I am Golden Hawk."

"But now you are my prisoner."

"Yes. For now."

For a long, uncertain moment Stalking Deer gazed down at Hawk. It was clear that Hawk's words had unsettled him and he was doing his best not to show it. Abruptly, without another word, Deer Stalker strode from the tepee.

Not long after, three braves entered, grabbed Hawk

by the feet, and dragged him from the chief's lodge, then tied him to a stake behind it. They checked the rawhide binding him, shortened the piece of rawhide connecting his wrists to his ankles, spat on him, and left.

For the remainder of that day, Hawk was the main attraction for the children and the old men and woman who came to torment him. The children pelted him with stones and horse turds and dug at him with sharpened sticks, while the women sliced out tiny pieces of the flesh on his back and arms. The bravest among them slashed off strands of his hair and fled with it, holding their trophies aloft triumphantly.

As dusk fell over the village, the Gros Ventre braves came by to kick him into insensibility. Hawk rolled into a ball and tried to absorb the punishment without complaint. At last, when weariness overtook his attackers, the braves drifted off to their tepees and a general silence fell over the village. A few dogs came to sniff at Hawk's battered body, then wandered off, bored.

As soon as he was alone, Hawk sat up and began to gnaw on the rawhide binding his wrists. He had been doing this furtively for most of the day, but the rawhide had dried nearly to the consistency of steel cable. Though he made some headway, it was too little to do him much good. Any real progress he might make would be discovered at once by his captors in the morning, and new, tighter bonds would immediately replace the old ones.

Still, it was his only hope, and like a feverish

beaver, he gnawed on the rawhide. So busy was he, he did not see Wild Flower until she had dropped down beside him. She had a heavy trade blanket with her and placed it down onto the ground for him. He moved gratefully onto it.

"You are very kind, Wild Flower."

"It is Deer Stalker you should thank. He tells me to do this. He say if I comfort you, perhaps you will not be so angry with him and his band for selling you to the Blackfoot. Then you will not send the buffalo into the deep canyons of fire. Is that true?"

"When you see him," Hawk said, "you tell him I appreciate the gesture, but tell him it is not enough. When I get my strength back, the Golden Hawk will swoop down and stampede every buffalo herd he sees into the fiery canyons of hell."

She shuddered and moved closer to him. "Can you do such a thing?"

"Have you not seen enough of the white man's magic to know he can do anything—no matter how terrible."

"But you would not make the buffalo disappear!"

"Maybe I won't," he said, "if you cut me loose."

"I have no knife."

"Untie me then."

"If I do that, Deer Stalker will know."

"Do it anyway."

"He will punish me. Perhaps he will kill me."

"All right then. Don't untie me. But be sure to tell Deer Stalker what I said. Soon, the buffalo herds will vanish forever into the white man's hell."

She shuddered, half convinced that Hawk, despite his present unhappy circumstances, was quite capable of carrying out his terrible threat. She moved closer, his awesome power filling her with terror— and something else. He felt her hot breath on his face. With his wrists still bound, he looped his arms over her shoulders and pulled her even closer. She responded eagerly and closed her moist lips over his, her tongue probing between them with sudden, reckless abandon.

He rolled over onto her, then pulled his mouth away from hers. "Dammit!" he told her hoarsely. "Help me get into you. I'm all tied up."

"No," she said, her teeth gleaming in the darkness. "I will not do that for you. It is good for me that you are tied. You will not fly away or devour me."

"Don't you bet on that," he told her, planting his lips fiercely over hers again.

Her fingers reached down swiftly to open his fly. As soon as it was open, she thrust herself under him and drove her thighs upward. His throbbing erection slipped into her warm moistness and he plunged fiercely down onto her, no longer aware of the rawhide shackling him. Her arms tightened about his neck and her mouth opened as she gasped with pleasure.

"Ah!" she cried. "Golden Hawk is a great bird who plunges deep into me. Go further still! Deeper!"

He did what he could to oblige until he was impaling her backside into the ground with each thrust. Tight, pleased grunts came from her as she met every thrust of his with one of her own. Soon they were slamming so fiercely against each other he wondered dimly if he was hurting her. But she did not pull back, and her fierce drive toward a climax only increased her wild, driving lunges up at him.

"Ah!" she cried suddenly, her fists hammering on him wildly. She flung her head back and cried out a second time, her entire body heaving up under him. Grunting himself, his own head flung back, he drove her back down onto the blanket as his own orgasm swept him along, his pulsing erection filling her with his hot seed. When he tried to pull out, she grabbed his thighs and kept him inside her while her muscles milked him for every remaining drop of seed.

"Now," she breathed, "I will have such fine sons the women of the band will bow to me when I pass! Their hair will be golden like yours and they will be just as fierce."

He pulled back to look down at her. "You goin' to let these Big Bellies sell the father of such famous sons to the filthy Blackfoot?"

"Do not worry," she said, pulling him down onto her. "It will be all right. Your sons will avenge you."

"I see. And I'll watch it all from the land beyond."

"Yes," she said, his irony lost on her.

"That will be little comfort."

"Then let this be comfort for you."

She bent to his crotch, her hot lips moving lightly into the hollow near his thigh bones, then over to close about the tip of his sagging member. Before long her ministrations had caused him to become erect once more, and this time she mounted him quickly, slamming herself down onto him with such enthusiasm, he was afraid she might break it off.

"It has been so long for me," she panted, brushing her hair back impatiently as he began to rock violently back and forth. "Deer Stalker is such an old man."

Hawk said nothing as he drove up to meet her thrusts, his big hands—still bound together—playing over first one nipple, then the other. She leaned forward, bracing herself on the ground on each side of his head, and let her breasts brush his face. Greedily, still thrusting upward, his lips closed about her large nipples and he hung on grimly.

At the last of it, he could hold off no longer and rolled her over onto her back, slamming into her with such fury, she cried out and then rolled him over once again so that she remained on top. They were off the blanket now, his back digging into the soft ground. But he did not care as they both climaxed, clawing at each other all the while. Sweat poured off both of them as she collapsed forward onto his chest, her lips covering it with kisses.

For him to be having such a good time under such miserable circumstances was crazy, Hawk realized. And then he found himself burying his face in the intoxicating perfume of her wild, black hair. She was still not done with him, he realized, her awakened hunger seemingly insatiable, and for an hour or so longer they kept at it, exploring each other's weaknesses and desires until at last she left him, and he lay back on the blanket she had brought him and fell into a deep, fathomless sleep.

Though Elias Hogwood had been cautious enough to camp in thick willows and had not even lit a fire the night before, when he awoke that morning, he found he had two Indian visitors—all the way from another planet, by the looks of them.

Bare-chested, dressed in breechclouts and moccasins that reached to their knees, they were short in stature, bowlegged, with wide, stocky bodies. They pushed through the willows cautiously, their raisin-black eyes staring down at him out of wide, impassive faces. That they had not killed him while he slept was a good sign. But he saw at once that they already must have found his tethered mounts, for one of them was holding the rifle he had taken from Golden Hawk.

The one holding the rifle limped slightly as he stepped closer to Hogwood. "Where you get this rifle?"he demanded.

Hogwood was startled at the question—and the English spoken by the Indian. It was English, all right, but with the hint in it of a southern or Texan drawl. His first instinct was right. These were Comanche, come all the way from Texas.

"Golden Hawk," Hogwood replied. "I got it from Golden Hawk. He gave it to me."

The Comanche stepped closer, brought the stock of the Hawken around swiftly, smashing the side of Hogwood's face and sending him tumbling clear of his blanket.

"Hey!" he cried, holding his hand up to his face. "I ain't got no quarrel with any Comanche!"

"Golden Hawk not give you this rifle!"

"All right! All right! I took it from him!"

"You take from Golden Hawk?" The Comanche was obviously astounded at such a possibility.

"Sure," Hogwood insisted. "I took it from him."

The Comanche's eyes narrowed. He leaned closer, even though Hogwood's stench obviously repelled him. "*You* killed Golden Hawk?"

"Well, no," Hogwood replied nervously. "Not exactly. I didn't kill the son-of-a-bitch. I traded him to the Gros Ventres and they gave him to the Blackfoot. They must've killed him by now. I'd say his hair is likely hangin' from a Blackfoot scalp pole."

"Blackfoot kill Golden Hawk?"

"That's right. Black Feather's band. Them Blackfoot devils don't like him worth shit."

The two Comanche looked at each other. They understood Hogwood only partially, he realized. He had seen disappointment first, then anger cross their faces. They must have come a long way to find the son-of-a-bitch, Hogwood realized. And then Hogwood recalled dimly the stories he had heard in trading posts and around campfires—wild tales of Comanche warriors coming all the way from Texas to find and kill Golden Hawk.

The two Comanche stared grimly down at him. In their cold glances Hogwood read a chilling resolve. If they couldn't have Golden Hawk's scalp, they were damned well going to take his as a consolation.

In that instant he realized he had been a fool to tell them Golden Hawk was dead.

He laughed. Loudly. The feigned madness he had used for so long as a defense against these credulous savages burst from him as easy as exhaling. Standing up, he flung his head back and laughed still more, his eyes wide, alight with madness. Alarmed, the two Comanche stepped back warily.

"Hell! I was just kiddin', fellers!" he told them. "The Golden Hawk ain't dead. You can't kill that one. I just said that to throw you off. Are you friends of his?"

The two Comanche thought a minute, trying to figure out this man in front of them. Then they nodded carefully. They were lousy liars, but that was all right with Hogwood.

"Why didn't you say you was friends? Why sure, Golden Hawk's all right! He left me with a load of furs just a while back and went home!"

"Home? Where?"

"To his cabin above the Snake. Yes sir, he's got himself a real fine Crow woman there. Raven Eyes. Before Golden Hawk went back, he let me borrow his rifle. He told me he has enough furs to get a new one at Fort Union."

Again the two Indians exchanged glances. Hogwood could see in their damned, heathen eyes what they were thinking. They didn't believe him. But they couldn't afford not to, either. If he was telling them the truth, they would find Golden Hawk on the Snake. If Hogwood was lying, Golden Hawk was already dead—and there was an end to it.

"I think you lie," said the Indian with the gimpy leg.

Hogwood shrugged. "Suit yourself."

"You stink."

"No need to get nasty about it. We all got our faults. Listen. Take that rifle of Hawk's. Sure, go ahead, take it. You can have it. Return it to Golden Hawk. Tell him I didn't need it."

The Comanche swung the rifle and this time caught Hogwood on the back of his head. Hogwood spun to the ground, the universe whirling sickeningly around him. He waited for the next blow. When it came, it was a moccasined foot that dug cruelly into his side. Then the Walker revolver was taken from him. The Indian stepped back, aimed it down at Hogwood, and fired. The big revolver's detonation was such that the Comanche almost dropped it. The slug slammed the side of Hogwood's head, glanced off, and burrowed into the ground.

But the force of the blow was enough to ring his noggin and send him plunging into darkness. The last thing he remembered hearing was the sound they made moving back through the willows. A moment later he heard the muffled thunder of their ponies as they rode off.

He breathed a deep sigh of relief and pushed himself to a sitting position. They had taken his ponies, he knew—but that didn't matter. They were heading south.

—— Chapter Seven ——

When Hawk awoke that same morning, he was shivering violently. His clothes were sopping wet from the heavy dew, and he had to clamp his jaw shut to stop his teeth from chattering.

Struggling to a sitting position on the blanket, he started flapping his arms in an effort to pump some warmth back into himself when he saw a white man in buckskin pants and a patched buckskin shirt coming toward him through the mists that still clung to the ground. He walked in a curious, hopping way and was carrying an earthen jug. Flopping down beside Hawk, the fellow held the jug of water out to Hawk and in a burr thick enough to cut with a knife, introduced himself as Angus MacDougal.

Hawk gulped the water down gratefully, then handed the jug back and took a long look at Angus MacDougal. The man's ruddy, bearded face was framed by unruly strands of greasy, reddish hair, and his alert eyes were a bright, china blue.

"Well, Angus," said Hawk, "What in blazes're you doin' here with these fat bellies?"

"I don't have much choice, laddie," he replied, pointing to his feet. The tips of his moccasins were missing and Hawk could see that all the man's toes had been lopped off. "I canna go far with such feet. These heathen bastards captured me five years ago. Since that unholy date I have taken a wife and sired a multitude of heathen brats, may God forgive me."

To Hawk the unhappy Scotsman cut a ludicrous figure, but he sure as hell looked no more silly than Hawk must have looked at that moment. He thought of Hogwood and simmered. The trapper was crazy, all right. As crazy as a fox.

"You got any idea which direction Hogwood took when he left here?"

"He went south, laddie—and in a big hurry."

"You mean the Big Bellies chased him out of here?"

Angus nodded. "Seems they don't like any man who would betray a warrior, especially one as famous as you." Angus sat back on his haunches and gazed with some amusement at Hawk. "Yes sir, you sure have a fearsome reputation among these heathen. I'm surprised you ain't sprouted wings already and flown away from here."

"I don't have wings, Angus—but I'm not stayin' around to wait for them Blackfoot to get here, either. You got any idea which Blackfoot tribe Deer Stalker sent his son to?"

"A Blood tribe close by. The Red Leg band."

"That'd be Black Feather's band."

"That's the one, laddie."

"Angus," Hawk told him curtly, "tonight you are going to cut me loose."

"Laddie, I canna' do that.'"

"Why in hell not?"

"The Gros Ventres would beat me to death—and in that endeavor my woman would lead all the rest."

"Then come with me."

"I can barely walk. If I were to return to civilization, I would be an embarrassment to the Hudson's Bay Company and become in the end a miserable beggar selling pencils on some street corner. At least these heathen see to it that my woman and I and all my brats are clothed and fed."

"Stay here then, but cut me free."

"I do not have a knife."

"My throwing-knife is inside Deer Stalker's lodge. It's hanging by his shield. Get it for me."

"I can't do that, laddie, but I will ask Walks-in-Water. She has a thing for you—or so my woman told me this morning."

"Tell her then."

He nodded unhappily. "That I will, laddie, I only wish I could do more."

"Then come with me. On a horse, you won't be a cripple. With special shoes, I'll bet you could walk good enough. You say you'd end up a begger if you fled here. Well, what in blazes are you now?"

Angus winced at Hawk's words. "Let me think it over, laddie."

At that moment a dark, overweight woman in a dirty buckskin dress—her black hair flying, her eyes shooting sparks—appeared from around Deer Stalker's lodge with a frying pan in her hand.

One glance at her and Angus jumped to his feet, tottered precariously for a moment, then hobbled off grotesquely, the woman flying after him, calling after him in a high, scolding screech. Watching the Scotsman flee before his termagant wife, Hawk shook his head. Despite his present difficulties, he was a lucky man.

A moment later Hawk's first visitor of the new day arrived—a gray-haired, snaggle-toothed hag with a freshly cut willow switch. Hitching up her dress, she began whipping him, cackling happily all the while. Hunching over, Hawk held his hands up to his eyes to protect them. As the old woman did her best to peel the skin off his hide, her breathing became labored, and she began to wheeze like a horse. But it did not deter her any, and when she left at last, keening happily, the younger women of the tribe arrived with their children to take up where she had left off. . . .

Soon after dusk, the cries of his tormentors still ringing in his ears, Hawk fell into a troubled sleep, every muscle and joint in his body aching, his back feeling like raw beefsteak. It was midnight when he awoke again. He could barely see, so swollen were his cheeks. Though his jaw still functioned, he had to work it carefully. Aside from this, all four of his limbs were serviceable, though he was still bound tightly, the rawhide digging cruelly into his wrists and ankles.

A shadow fell over him. He looked up to see Wild

Flower. She bent beside him and, with Hawk's own throwing-knife, sliced through the rawhide holding his wrists. Then she handed his knife to him. Reaching down with it, he cut through the rawhide to free his ankles, gritting his teeth as he endured the sharp bout of pins and needles caused by the blood rushing back into his feet. Wild Flower bent to massage them while he rubbed his hands together.

Finally he was able to stand. Wild Flower helped him to keep erect, then glanced past him. She gasped. Hawk turned. Deer Stalker was standing behind him, his war club in one hand, a huge knife in the other.

"Now I kill Golden Hawk," Deer Stalker told him, "so his medicine will not send all the buffalo to hell!"

As the chief brought his war club down, Hawk ducked aside. The club glanced off his shoulder, but the blow was still powerful enough to drive him to one knee. Brandishing his knife, the chief moved in to finish Hawk off. But Wild Flower blocked his way, grabbing frantically for the chief's knife hand as she did so. But she was no match for the chief. He slashed contemptuously at her with his knife and caught her in the side.

Wild Flower cried out and collapsed to the ground. But she had given Hawk time to recover. He hurled himself at Deer Stalker and drove him back, slamming him to the ground. As Deer Stalker hit, Hawk brushed aside the chief's knife hand and buried his throwing-knife deep into the chief's chest. Gasping, the chief bucked violently under Hawk, attempting to dislodge him. Hawk brought his knife down again, this time slicing clear to the chief's heart. The old man's powerful body heaved, then with a deep sigh settled under him.

Hawk got slowly, wearily to his feet, not one bit happy at having killed the chief. In spite of everything, Hawk had come to like him. In one thing at least, the two sure as hell thought alike.

Both of them hated the white man's towns.

Hawk helped Wild Flower back onto her feet. "Are you all right?" he asked. Her dress below the wound in her side was already dark with blood.

"It is nothing," Wild Flower told him, tearing a strip from the bottom of her dress. As she wrapped it around her waist to stop the bleeding, she stepped closer to the dead chief and looked down at him in some awe.

"Is the old fool really dead?"

"He didn't give me much of a choice. And if you hadn't done what you did, he might have finished me. Thanks, Wild Flower."

"What will you do now?"

"Get out of here—and as fast as I can."

"Then I come too!" Wild Flower told him. "I cannot stay here now. You must return me to my people."

"All right, Wild Flower. I guess I owe you."

"We go now?"

"First I need weapons." He lifted the dead chief and draped him over his shoulders, then headed for the tepee. "Is the chief's wife asleep in here?"

"Yes. I go with you. If she wake up, I will fix her."

"Go easy on her," Hawk cautioned. "We've already made her a widow."

Wild Flower glanced impatiently at Hawk. "Why should I be easy with her? She is never easy with me."

Hawk shrugged and carried the dead chief past her into the lodge. Unfolding him as gently as he could onto his couch, Hawk pulled a blanket over the dead body and glanced at the chief's widow. She was still asleep on her couch, her head turned the other way. Just in case, Wild Flower stood over her, one of the chief's war clubs in her hand. Hawk took down the chief's bow and quiver of arrows, and his rawhide reata. Then he nodded to Wild Flower and left the tepee, Wild Flower on his heels.

"We go now?" she whispered, her face white, strained. He looked at her waist. The strip of doeskin she had wrapped about her waist was already dark with her blood.

"We won't get very far afoot," he told her. "We need horses."

"When No-Toes send me to you with your knife, he say he will have ponies waiting across the river."

"Whereabouts?"

"There," she said, pointing. "In the willows."

"Let's go, then."

Angus was not only waiting with the ponies, he was astride one of them, eager to make his escape with Hawk.

"You were right laddie," he said, tossing to Hawk the ponies' reins. "On the back of a horse, I'm as good as any damned Big Belly. Now, if I can just ride this horse into a saloon, I will be one happy man.''

The Gros Ventre ponies Angus had secured were sturdy enough, and though the saddles were Indian, this was no problem for Hawk. He swung onto a powerful roan and led Angus and Wild Flower out of the willows. Soon they had left the canyon behind and were heading west across the plains, moving steadily toward the pile of peaks dimly visible on the night's horizon.

Hawk figured they had until daybreak to reach the timbered foothills of the Rockies before the Gros Ventre warriors mounted a pursuit. Since Hawk had left a dead chief behind, there was no doubt in his mind that there would be a pursuit—and a tenacious one at that.

But his real worry now was Wild Flower. For in spite of what she had told him, Deer Stalker had wounded her far more seriously than she was willing to admit; and at the moment she was leaving behind a spoor no Gros Ventre warrior could fail to spot.

Her own fresh blood.

At sunup, before they reached the timber, Hawk turned aside and rode up onto a hogback. Halting on the crest, he stood up on his saddle and peered back at the distant horizon. It took a long while for his eyes to pick out the faint, wavering dots that hovered over the shimmering horizon. He counted five riders in all, and once he was certain this was all the Gros Ventres were sending after them, he dropped back down onto his saddle and rode hard to overtake Angus and Wild Flower.

They reached the timbered foothills by midday. There Hawk and Angus did their best to bind up Wild Flower's wound and stanch her bleeding, after which they kept on until dusk, then camped by a mountain stream. By this time Wild Flower was in considerable pain. As they pressed on during the afternoon, it had not been easy for Hawk or Angus to ignore her discomfort. Now, by the light of their small campfire, Hawk examined Wild Flower's wound for the second time. Despite their efforts to close it and stanch the flow of blood, it still gaped open, its raw edges a feverish red. Wild Flower was not getting any better, Hawk realized, and she would not until they gave her a chance to rest.

"How far do you think we are from Flathead villages?" Hawk asked Wild Flower.

"I do not know," she replied. "It is not yet time for my people to make winter camp."

"We'll just have to keep going, then," he told her. "I'm sorry."

She smiled wanly, understanding perfectly their dilemma. After a moment she leaned her head back and passed out, as much from exhaustion as from her wound.

The next morning when they set out, Wild Flower seemed a little better. During the day, Hawk ranged ahead in search of game. With the bow and arrows he had stolen from Stalking Deer, Hawk managed to bring down a small deer, and that evening the three of them dined on fresh venison. The raw liver was saved for Wild Flower, who devoured it gratefully, after which she dropped once again into a deep sleep.

Three days later they found the Flatheads.

Around midmorning, entering a broad, wooded valley, they were suddenly confronted by six mounted warriors. The Indians had drifted out of the timbered slopes around them as silently as smoke. For a moment it looked like trouble as—their faces hard with resolve—the warriors slipped their bowstrings into the notches of their arrows and prepared to lift their bows. Then Wild Flower saved the situation. Breaking past Angus and Hawk, she rode eagerly toward one of the warriors.

"Crooked Arrow!" she cried. "Brother!"

At once the Flathead warrior recognized his sister, and slipping from his pony as she pulled up beside him, he lifted her down and they embraced.

As soon as they reached Crooked Arrow's village, an old medicine woman was called to his lodge to see to Wild Flower's wound. She washed out the wound thoroughly, then sewed up the long gash, packed against it a pungent poultice of dried leaves and herbs, then bade Wild Flower rest. Holding on to the old woman's hand, Wild Flower leaned back and slept.

Outside the lodge, Hawk and Angus—the Scotsman seemed to be getting around more easily each day—spoke to Crooked Arrow about the possibility that their Gros Ventre pursuers might still be on their trail.

"How many follow you?"

"I counted five."

"For Gros Ventre, that is large war party."

"Well, I don't want them to find Wild Flower again—or this village. It ain't just the Gros Ventres you've got to worry about, it's their allies, the Blackfoot."

"We know," Crooked Arrow said. "But we are not afraid of the Blackfoot or their fat-belly allies."

"That's good news, Crooked Arrow. How come?"

"Because already we have crossed over the mountains and hunted our buffalo on the Blackfoot plains. Now we have enough meat for the winter and plenty of skins too."

"How'd you manage that?" Angus asked.

Crooked Snake shrugged. "We hunt the buffalo before any other tribe, before the cows are ready for kill. Before rutting season."

No wonder, Hawk thought. He had noticed the stores of freshly killed buffalo, the racks of drying meat that now filled the gaps between the tepees. Everywhere Hawk looked, women were pounding on strips of pemmican or scraping clean the buffalo hides they would be trading at Fort Union later that fall.

"That was smart," Hawk agreed. "Sneaking onto the plains like that, before any other bands—but that only means you've got a lot to lose if those Gros Ventres spot this village and bring their Blackfoot allies in here. Looks to me like this here village of yours is especially vulnerable right now. You could lose all you've put aside for the winter."

Crooked Arrow frowned. "What you say would be bad for our people. Will Golden Hawk help?"

"I want to meet with your camp chief. Who is he?"

"Bear Claw."

"Tell him I have a plan."

Crooked Arrow hurried off to find the chief.

Later that same day he returned to Hawk with the news that a meeting had been arranged and was to take place in Bear Claw's lodge that same day. When Hawk arrived, he found Bear Claw—his short sturdy figure resplendent in robes, his graying hair freshly braided and decorated with ribbons—waiting eagerly for him.

But before any discussion could begin, the other Flathead chiefs and noted warriors of the band crowded in after Hawk, eager to participate in this momentous council with the famed Golden Hawk—the near-legendary white Comanche who now professed friendship with the Flathead people. Since to be host to such a momentous council gave Bear Claw enormous prestige, he did nothing to discourage the warriors crowding into his lodge.

At last, with his lodge close to bursting, Bear Claw gave a solemn speech of welcome. At its conclusion, other chiefs and warriors got gravely to their feet and followed suit. The custom, as Hawk knew, was for each speaker to be allowed his say, and only when all had spoken would it be Hawk's turn. Reasonably fluent with the Flathead tongue, Hawk had little difficulty following the debate that ensued.

Most of the speakers voiced the hope that Hawk would join them in their troubles with the Blackfoot in the belief that his medicine would prove a powerful weapon against them. Some even hoped Hawk's presence among them would halt further incursions on the villages. They knew by now that Hawk was in flight from the Gros Ventre village, but Hawk's reputation seemed only enhanced when it was learned he had killed Chief Stalking Deer, an old and wily enemy to the Flatheads.

Despite Hawk's reputation, however, a few of the shrewder chiefs expressed reservations about Hawk's value as a weapon against the Blackfoot. They pointed out that—despite Golden Hawk's fearsome reputation—he was only one man. And a white man, at that. Furthermore, the fact that he was a persistent enemy of the hated Blackfoot might only serve to draw the full wrath of the entire Blackfoot confederation down upon them. Increased pressure from their Blackfoot enemies, these speakers pointed out, they did not need.

At last, when the smoke in Bear Claw's crowded lodge had become thick enough to cut, it was Hawk's turn to address the members of the council. He began by thanking them all for their hospitality and reminding them that he had just returned Wild Flower to her own people. He went on to point out that his friendship with the Flatheads was strong, pointing out that he had never taken a Flathead scalp—or wanted to. The formalities over, Hawk calmly announced that he was in complete agreement with those who counseled against letting him stay in the village as a shield against the Blackfoot. It would cause trouble for the Flatheads, he admitted freely, and this Hawk would not abide.

This forthright statement caused an immediate stir, and those chiefs who had pushed such a view leaned back in some satisfaction, glancing about them and nodding sagely to others of their persuasion.

"Five Big Belly warriors have followed us from their village," Hawk continued. "They are eager to avenge the death of their chief. Soon they will find this village. Though any two Flathead braves are a match for any five Big Belly warriors, if any of these warriors escape, it is almost certain they will return to this village with their Blackfoot allies."

Troubled nods greeted this statement, and a worried, restless murmur passed around the lodge. Hawk held up his hand for silence, then continued.

"I will go from your village now," he told them. "And when I find these Gros Ventre warriors, I will lead them away from this village. All I ask from my Flathead brothers are such weapons as I will need to defend myself, provisions, and fresh ponies to take me on my way."

Finished, Hawk sat down.

Bear Claw stood up and turned to address Hawk. "Which direction will you take these Big Bellies?"

"North—into Blood country."

"Why would you do such a foolish thing?"

"I have a score to settle with Black Feather of the Blood tribe."

"Black Feather is a brave warrior. He has counted many coups."

"I will have his scalp—or he will have mine."

A murmur swept the ring of chiefs and warriors. Bear Claw sat down.

Another chief stood up to speak. "Golden Hawk is a brave and fierce warrior. But does he not wish

Flathead warriors to accompany him when he leaves
this village to meet the Gros Ventres?"

"No," Hawk replied. "It will not be necessary."

Another chief got to his feet then, solemnly fold-
ing his blanket over his shoulder as he did so. His
face was stern, his anthracite eyes gleaming as he
gazed upon Hawk. "It seems Golden Hawk has much
to do and many enemies to prevent him from doing
it. But this chief will gladly present two of his
finest war ponies to see him on his way. When will
Golden Hawk leave?"

"Today. Before nightfall."

A sigh of relief seemed to sweep the lodge. At
once others shot to their feet to add their contribu-
tions. When the members of the council streamed
finally from Bear Claw's tepee, Hawk found that
along with the two war ponies, he had been offered
a small arsenal and provisions enough to keep him
in blackfoot country for a long campaign. He was
pleased; and when Angus tottered up to him outside Bear Claw's lodge to ask how it went, Hawk
grinned and slapped the Scotsman on the back.

"It went as I thought it would," Hawk told him.
"They are so eager to get rid of me, they offered me
all I need—and more."

"Then you're still pulling out today?"

Hawk nodded.

"Well, then, so am I."

"You're crazy, Angus. You've already lost all your
toes. Do you want your scalp to follow?"

"Listen, laddie. I ain't much good afoot, but I'm
gettin' a whole lot better. And I got a score to settle
with them heathen who done this to me. If I don't

go with you, why I'll just go back and meet them alone."

"No need for that, Angus. We'll ride out together."

Wild Flower was fully awake when Hawk ducked into Crooked Arrow's lodge to say good bye to her. She was sitting up, while an Indian girl spooned soup into her. Her eyes were clear and most of the color had returned to her cheeks. It was obvious that the Flathead medicine woman knew her business. Wild Flower was on the mend.

"You look fine," Hawk said, looking down at her.

"I feel much better."

"Angus and I are pulling out now," he told her. "We wish you luck."

"You will return, Golden Hawk?"

"Perhaps."

"You must return to see your golden son. I am sure there will be one. It is what I want."

"If I can, I will."

That seemed to satisfy her. Wild Flower then glanced at Angus and smiled. "You walk almost like grown man again. I am glad to see this. Fight well by Golden Hawk's side."

"I'll do that, Wild Flower. That's a promise."

Wild Flower nodded and turned her head to face the Indian girl who had been feeding her. The audience was concluded. There was no more to be said. The two men left the lodge.

The afternoon sun was still slanting down through the pines when Hawk and Angus rode out of the Flathead village. In response to Hawk's plea for weapons, Bear Claw had presented Hawk with a bowie knife and a huge flintlock pistol altered for percussion caps. Crooked Arrow had given him a flintlock rifle along with plenty of shot and powder. Nor had Angus been left out. One of the chiefs had presented him with a handsome, long-barrel breech-loading Kentucky rifle.

They headed back the way they had come, keeping to the slopes above the trail, and as dusk fell they made a dry camp high in the timber and lit no fire, content to chew on the pemmican they had been given. Meanwhile, so much store did Angus put by the Kentucky rifle given to him, he was still cleaning it by the light of the moon when Hawk fell asleep.

The next day they continued back along the trail, still keeping to the slopes above it. A little before midday they spotted the five Gros Ventre warriors. Dismounting, they peered through the timber at them. The five warriors were making good time, only they were riding back the way they had come.

"You hit it right on the nose, laddie," Angus said. "They're on their way back to tell what they found not far from here."

"And as far as they know, I'm still in that Flathead village."

"That's all the excuse they'd need to attack it."

Hawk nodded. "Them and their Blackfoot allies."

"So what do we do now?"

Hawk pointed to a high, wooded ridge on the trail half a mile ahead of the Indians. "Get back up on that pony and ride ahead. Get to that ridge before they do. Then wait from me to open up."

"We ain't likely to get them all," Angus pointed out.

"I know that. But we'll whittle them down some."

Angus groped carefully back to his pony, pulled himself into the saddle, and took off up the slope. In a moment he had disappeared into the timber. Hawk mounted up also and rode ahead through the timber. Then he let his pony take him down the timbered slope until he was closing fast on the unsuspecting warriors.

When they were almost below the ridge where Angus should have been waiting, Hawk dismounted, charged his flintlock, then ran swiftly down through the timber until he was within a hundred yards of the five. They were talking loudly as they rode, evidently trying to decide on a spot to rest up. The Gros Ventre nearest to Hawk was a big fellow sitting lazily back on his fat pony. Hawk tracked him carefully and squeezed the trigger. The flintlock misfired. A sudden flame leaped up from the pan, nearly blinding him. The effect was worthless, the noise considerable, and all he had succeeded in doing was alerting the five warriors.

Flinging the rifle to the ground, Hawk raced down through the timber toward them, fitting the notch of his arrow to his bowstring as he ran. The warrior he had taken aim on had turned his pony about and was now galloping full-tilt back toward Hawk. Hawk kept on nevertheless, and once clear of the timber, he held up, aimed, and let fly. His arrow caught the Gros Ventre full in the chest, knocking him backward off his horse. At that moment Angus opened up from the ridge, his rifle considerably more reliable than Hawk's. A warrior in the act of wheeling his pony around to come after Hawk flung up his arms and peeled off his saddle.

The remaining three warriors—aware they were caught in a crossfire—lashed their ponies off the trail and disappeared into the timber.

Done with scalping the two dead warriors, Angus mounted up and rode over to where Hawk was examining his rifle. It was useless, Hawk concluded, beyond repair. He flung it to one side.

"You can have mine if you want it," said Angus. From the look on his face, Hawk could tell it was the last thing Angus wanted.

Hawk grinned up at him. "Keep it. I still have a bow and arrow—and this revolver."

"You sure that'll be enough?"

"Yes."

Obviously relieved, Angus said, "Let's go then, before them three get far."

"They're already far. You go on to Fort Union, Angus. I don't need you for what I got ahead of me."

"You mean you work better alone."

"Yes."

"If that's the way you want it."

"Just don't let any Piegans see those fresh Gros Ventre scalps hanging from your belt."

He grinned. "I won't."

"And you can do me a favor."

"Name it, Hawk."

"I got a cabin on the Snake, near Fort Hall. Check it out for me, will you? I been gone a long time. There's a woman might be there, waiting for me. Her name's Raven Eyes. Tell her I won't be long."

"You still goin' after Black Feather?"

Hawk nodded.

"Well, I hope you're right—that you won't be long, I mean."

"If I don't get back before winter closes in, see to Raven Eyes for me. Maybe you and that Kentucky rifle will be able to put food on her table."

"I'll do that, laddie, but I'm figurin' on you showing up before the first snow flies."

Hawk nodded. "I'll be there."

With a quick wave, the Scotsman turned his pony and set off. Hawk watched until he was out of sight beyond the ridge; then he mounted up and set off after the remaining Gros Ventre warriors. He figured they would be a mite nervous now, knowing they were the hunted. He was sure of it when he saw how straight their line of flight was. He kept on, catching up to them a little after dark. They had been foolish enough to build a campfire.

Smiling, Hawk tethered his pony and closed in.

—— Chapter Eight ——

The Gros Ventre brave sitting closest to Hawk was an unusually thin Indian, at least for a Gros Ventre. He sat cross-legged on his blanket, smoking his pipe, his gaze fixed on the dark outline of the distant hills. The other two Indians were not immediately visible. Only when Hawk crept closer to the campfire could he see their dark forms sitting on the grass beyond it. They were arguing heatedly over something.

His head down, his body moving almost imperceptibly through the tall grass, Hawk was within twenty-five yards of them when one of the Indians on the other side of the fire stood up and marched off toward a fairly steep ridge. The two had been arguing about who was going to be the camp sentry that night, it appeared. Moving backward with extreme caution, Hawk regained the cover of the steep, timbered slope, then moved up it until he was able to approach the ridge from above. Hawk crept to within twenty feet of the camp's sentry and lay perfectly still in the tall grass and waited.

By midnight the campfire below was no more than a patch of glowing embers sitting in the dark void of the valley floor, and the two Indians had long since curled up in their blankets beside it. The lone sentry, his head bowed forward over his crossed legs, was now fast asleep. Hawk rose from the grass, ran the remaining few yards to the sleeping Indian, and dropped the reata's noose around his neck. Snapping it shut with swift, brutal finality, he dragged the garroted Indian off the knoll and into the timber.

He had already selected his pine tree, and climbing rapidly into its topmost branches, he wedged the dead Indian between two of them and clambered down. Breaking off two branches, he dragged them deeper into the timber, their twin furrows aping those made earlier by the dead Indian's heels. He left off in deep brush, tossed the branches into a ravine, and slipped back down through the timber to the stream below the Indians' camp, where they had tethered their ponies. With one slice of his knife, Hawk cut through the rope corral and simply by raising his hands sent the spooked ponies galloping off down the trail, the muffled thunder of their unshod hooves fading almost at once. Returning to his own mount, Hawk rode as high as he could on the steep slope above the Indian camp, dismounted on a well-protected ridge, and wrapping himself in his soogan, fell instantly asleep.

As he knew it would, the sound of cries from the camp below awakened Hawk at dawn. He watched as the two Gros Ventres raced down the slope to where they had left their ponies. It did not take them long to find the neatly sliced rope. Almost as an afterthought, they ran up the slope toward the ridge, calling out to their missing sentry.

Once on the ridge, they followed the spoor Hawk had deliberately left and soon disappeared into the timber. By this time Hawk had already mounted up, confident the Indians would not find their companion's body where he had hidden it. Riding on ahead, he halted on a slope a mile or so distant, one that gave him a long view of the trail below him—and waited for the two Gros Ventres, now afoot, to appear.

When the two Indians did come in sight, they were stumbling pathetically along, obviously hoping to overtake their ponies. Keeping in the timber well above the trail, Hawk had no difficulty keeping up with them. When darkness closed in, the two Indians were careful this time not to build a fire.

Once Hawk was certain the two had bedded down for the night, he rode back, retrieved the dead Indian, slung him across his pony's neck, and rode back with him. Leaning the corpse against a tree on a ridge high above the spot where the Indians slept, Hawk vanished into the timber and prepared to add more fuel to his legend.

By midnight he was ready. A gleaming full moon hung above the trail, giving him all the light he needed. After testing the reata to make sure it would hold his weight, he crouched low in the shadow of a tall pine, cupped his hand about his mouth, and uttered a high, unearthly screech that ended in a long, terrible wail—the call of the terrible and universally feared Cannibal Owl.

Hawk saw the two Indians spring up from their blankets. Moving into the shadows beside the propped-up Indian, Hawk let go with another high, looping screech. One of the Indians pointed up at the pale face of the dead Indian gazing mutely down the moonlit slope at them. For a moment they stood transfixed at the sight. Then, despite what must have been fearsome misgivings, they left the ridge and clambered swiftly up the steep slope toward their dead comrade.

When they were within twenty feet of their dead companion— tottering on the edge of the steep slope, their faces white with terror—Hawk let out one more terrible screech, then flung himself out of the shadows at them, the winglike network of pine branches he had attached to his shoulders flaring like the wings of some monstrous night hawk. Clinging to the reata with both hands, Hawk's chest struck the closest Indian, bowling him back against his companion, sending them both crashing head over heels down the slope. Still clinging to the reata, Hawk swept out over the trail in a long, circular arc, uttering one more terrible cry before he swooped around and vanished back into the timber. Dropping lightly to the ground, he hurried to the edge of the timber and looked down. One of the Indians—crazed with fear—was running off through the moonlit darkness. In seconds, he was out of sight.

The other Indian was sprawled at the bottom of the slope. From the look of his twisted body, Hawk was almost certain the precipitous plunge had severely injured or possibly killed him. He loosened, then flung aside the branches he had used for his deception and angled swiftly down the slope.

But just as Hawk reached him, the fallen Indian stirred, then sat up. Pulling his knife, he slashed hastily up at Hawk. Hawk twisted aside, evading the gleaming blade, then backed up and began to circle the Indian warily. The Indian tried repeatedly to get up, but each time he fell back, favoring his left leg. Peering closely at the leg, Hawk saw it was bent cruelly just above the ankle. A white splinter of bone protruded through the flesh, gleaming in the moonlight like a fang. Hawk had the advantage, surely. Stepping closer, he reached out with his own blade, jabbing tauntingly at the Indian's midsection.

Incredibly, despite his shattered leg, the Indian forced himself to stand unaided, then made a desperate lunge for Hawk, his knife slashing out wickedly. Hawk stepped aside, easily evading the blade as the warrior stumbled past him, then crashed headlong to the ground. As the warrior flung himself over to face him, Hawk took a single step forward and kicked the knife tightly and gathered himself to finish off the disarmed warrior.

But something deep inside him held him back—would not let him do it. Slowly, he lowered his knife.

"Go ahead, Golden Hawk," the warrior taunted, "I am waiting."

"No," Hawk told him, stepping back. "You have too great a heart to die like this.'

"You mock me. Already you have killed my brother, Hungry Fox. I will follow him to the Sand Hills."

"Later. You have plenty of time for that journey."

The warrior glanced down at his shattered left leg. "This ankle hangs like a broken twig. I will have to chop it off. I will be a warrior no more. Like a dog hoping for scraps, I will wait for others to return from their raids. And what woman would have a cripple for a husband? Kill me Golden Hawk. If you can."

Hawk sheathed his knife and knelt beside the warrior, realizing he was the same one he had watched earlier puffing on his pipe and gazing raptly into the distance. For a moment Hawk thought the desperate warrior would strike out at him, but the moment passed and he took the warrior under his arms and pulled him gently closer to the stream, resting him back against the trunk of a cottonwood tree.

"Take out your pipe and light it," Hawk suggested. "I am going to set this leg of yours."

"Is Golden Hawk a medicine man who fixes broken bones?"

"His medicine is very powerful," Hawk acknowledged, and caught a glint of amusement in the warrior's eyes.

As Hawk poked about in the darkness for lengths of dried wood he could use for splints, the warrior took out his pipe and fumbling open his tobacco pouch, thumbed tobacco into the bowl. He had some trouble lighting the pipe with his flintstone, but as soon as he got the pipe drawing to his satisfaction, he nodded his readiness to Hawk.

During his years with the Kwahadi Comanches, Hawk had witnessed many falls from ponies and seen quite a few braves snap a leg in the process. Setting the leg was always a painful business, but one thing he had learned in watching the process was that it had to be quick and decisive—if the limb was to be saved. Better a poor bone alignment that a drawn-out, crippling attempt to match the bone fragments perfectly, for such indecisiveness only caused bones to splinter and vital ligaments to tear.

Keeping this in mind, Hawk clasped one hand firmly about the Indian's shin above the break, then took his ankle just as firmly with the other. He waited for the Indian to take the pipe stem from his mouth and yanked the ankle down, then twisted, letting go to let the ligaments snap the broken bone together. The Indian's cry was short, and when Hawk looked up, he saw he had passed out, the smoking pipe on the ground beside him, the still-glowing tobacco having spilled across the dark ground.

Hawk felt the bone alignment. It was not perfect, but it was better than he had expected, and moistening a portion of his reata in the stream, he wrapped it about the wood splints he held in place about the leg. When he had finished, there was no way the Indian could flex the ankle and from the knee down the leg was completely immobilized. Whether the Indian ever regained full use of his leg was up to chance and chance alone. And he would need a special brand of luck if he was to escape infection at the point where the bone splinter had broken through.

Hawk left the Indian to go after his pony. He was not happy that in deciding to save this Gros Ventre's leg he would more than likely be unable to overtake the third Indian. By dawn the fleeing warrior would be out of these foothills, well on his way back across the plains to his village. But unless he overtook the ponies, he would be afoot all the way, and Hawk could easily overtake him; but Hawk's first responsibility now was to see to this Gros Ventre. To abandon him in these hills untended and without food or a horse would mean a death as certain as a well-aimed bullet.

When he rode back to the stream, he found the Gros Ventre had regained consciousness. It was not yet dawn and Hawk was exhausted. He left the Indian by the cottonwood, tethered his pony about half a mile upstream, then secured a few hours of sleep in a well-hidden spot high in the timber.

Hawk still had his scalp when he awoke. He rode back to the Gros Ventre. They managed a meager breakfast from Hawk's store of provisions. Afterward, the Gros Ventre offered no objection when Hawk boosted him up onto Hawk's pony, while Hawk walked alongside. The two conversed and Hawk learned that his prisoner was called Running Bear. Jokingly, the Indian suggested he might soon change it to Lame Bear.

When they stopped at noon to rest and slake their thirst, Running Bear allowed himself to be helped off the horse by Hawk, then leaned back against a tree as Hawk made coffee and fried some jerky. When they had rested, Running Bear put aside his cup and looked curiously at Hawk.

"Why does Golden Hawk help Running Bear? He cares for him like a brother. Is he not the feared and terrible Cannibal Owl?"

"Only on moonlit nights," Hawk told him.

"Then you are only a man like any other."

"That's what everyone says," Hawk admitted ruefully. He finished filling his pipe, then lit up with a faggot from the fire. "Except—like I said—on moonlit nights."

"You are a fool, Golden Hawk."

"Why?"

"Because you think helping this warrior will soften me. It will not. I am still waiting to kill you as soon as I get the chance."

Hawk shrugged. "I expect that from a warrior as courageous as you. If I thought any different, I would not bother to help you."

Considering this, Running Bear puffed quietly on his pipe for a while longer, then turned to gaze coldly on Hawk. "I am glad you understand, Golden Hawk. What you do for me changes nothing. You may be Golden Hawk or the great Cannibal Owl. It does not matter. It is all the same to me. You are an ally of the hated Flatheads. You have killed one of my comrades. When this leg is healed, I will come for you."

"And I'll be waiting, Running Bear."

"Perhaps you will not have to wait long."

Hawk glanced down at the Indian's leg. So far there was no sign that the bone had broken through the flesh again, and another good sign was that the Indian was not feverish. "My hope is that your recovery will be complete, that as you say, we will not have long to wait. As soon as you have two good legs under you again, I look forward to the honor of facing you in combat."

Running Bear did not respond, but his eyes gleamed in appreciation of Hawk's words—and in the anticipation of future combat, Hawk had no doubt.

It was clear to Hawk that under different circumstances both men might have become comrades in arms, for Running Bear was a warrior with a great heart, as Hawk had noted earlier. He was a man to stand with against one's enemies.

Hawk was leading the pony through the last of the foothills, Running Bear slumped wearily over the saddle horn, when from out behind a clump of birch rode a lone Blackfoot. At sight of him, Hawk released the bridle, drew his pistol, and stepped out in front of the pony to see what this warrior wanted.

What he wanted was trouble.

Letting out a high, whooping war cry, he spurred his pony toward Hawk. Fully alert on the instant, Running Bear saw his chance. Spurring past Hawk, he wheeled the pony and lifted it to a sudden gallop, intent on running Hawk down. Turning to face him, Hawk aimed his pistol at Running Bear and fired point-blank.

The pistol misfired and a second later the pony's head and neck slammed into Hawk, flinging him backward. He struck the ground and just managed to roll out from under the pony's hooves, its belly sailing over his head. Dazed, he got up onto one knee. Once again the pounding of unshod hooves grew louder behind him and he turned to see Running Bear bearing down on him a second time. Jumping up, he dodged aside, reached up, and grabbed Running Bear's splinted leg. Clinging to it, he hauled the Indian off the hard-charging pony.

As Running Bear landed on his back, his cry rent the air. Hawk let go of the broken leg and swung around to meet the Blackfoot. He had leaped from his saddle by this time and was now running swiftly toward him with drawn knife. Hawk drew his own knife and braced himself just as Running Bear flung his forearm over Hawk's head and pressed it back against his windpipe.

In pure agony, Hawk dropped his knife and sagged to the ground, trying desperately to pry himself free of Running Bear's viselike grip. That was when the other warrior arrived to finish Hawk. Letting loose with another war cry, his painted face distorted with fury, the Blackfoot lifted his knife high above his head.

Before he could bring it down, however, an arrow head burst through his chest wall. The knife fell from his fingers and he collapsed face down in the grass beside Hawk. A sudden cry exploded behind Hawk. Running Bear's forearm loosened from his throat. Tiny lights danced before his eyes as Hawk, fighting for air, rolled free of Running Bear and glanced behind him. The shaft of a Flathead arrow was protruding from Running Bear's side, and both his hands were clasped about it as he tugged futilely on it. He glanced at Hawk as if to ask for help.

Hawk got to his feet and stepped back coldly, watching.

Running Bear pitched forward to the ground—a dead man.

Hawk glanced in the direction from which both arrows had come and saw an old comrade on a spotted pony break from the timber and ride toward him.

Two Scalps.

── Chapter Nine ──

Around a campfire that night, while both Hawk and Two Scalps smoked their pipes, Hawk explained how he had managed to find himself fighting off a Gros Ventre warrior and a Blackfoot at the same time. After listening to Hawk's explanation, Two Scalps shook his head, an amused gleam in his obsidian eyes.

"You fix Gros Ventre's leg," he summarized. "So then he thank you and try to kill you. Next time do not wait. Finish Indian. Never mind how brave he is." He chuckled. "Golden Hawk is maybe not such a fierce and terrible bird, after all."

Hawk nodded gloomily. "I guess I'll just have to get meaner."

"And take fewer gifts," Two Scalps said, reminding Hawk of the useless firearms given him by the Flatheads.

Hawk leaned back and tried to digest the wild events of that day. Though Two Scalps had wanted to take Running Bear's scalp, Hawk had restrained him. Having done what he could to save Running

Bear's leg, Hawk still felt a crazy sense of responsibility for him.

Hawk wondered if Two Scalps was right—that he was maybe losing his edge. Was Hawk no longer a very fierce or terrible bird, after all?

"You are still heading north," Two Scalps remarked, taking the pipe from his mouth.

"Yes."

"Two moons north of here is a Blood village."

"I know."

"It is Black Feather you seek?"

"Yes."

Two Scalps puffed for a while on his pipe, then took the stem from his mouth and glanced sidelong at Hawk. "I seek him also. It is his band which destroyed my village. Which of us will take his scalp?"

"We will decide that when the time comes."

"Yes, when we capture him."

"Capture him?"

Two Scalps nodded grimly. "Yes. We will take him alive. For such a warrior, a quick death would be too easy on him. We will see in what manner his soul enters the Sand Hills."

Two Scalps stuck his pipe back into his mouth. Hawk leaned back and said nothing more. There was little left to say and much ahead to do.

The Blood village was strung out below them in a wooded ravine, following along beside a narrow, swift-moving stream. Birch and cottonwood lined both its banks, the lodges of the Blood band constructed among the timber. The women were as usual the most active, collecting firewood, hauling water, or standing in the stream's shallows, beating the dickens out of their clothing. Between the lodges streamed the gangs of shrill, uncontrollable Indian youngsters. The village's pony herd was in sight farther up the ravine, its ranks visibly swelling with the stock the band's warriors had taken from Two Scalps' village and the wagon train. But there were many lodges without ponies tethered in front of them, and a large percentage of the braves visible were old chiefs wrapped in blankets, their white hair blowing thinly in the wind.

Two Scalps noticed this at once. "I do not see many warriors," he commented.

"And I do not see Black Feather."

"We will have to wait," Two Scalps said. "Black Feather is off with a war party."

Hawk nodded, aware that Black Feather might not have returned yet from the Gros Ventre village where he had gone to trade for Golden Hawk. This was surprising, since the Gros Ventre village was supposedly not that far from this band's camp. The two men pushed back through the grass, mounted up, and rode off into a high patch of timber, where they made camp for the night.

They had only just settled down in their blankets when they heard the rapid, excited beat of drums. Getting up hurriedly, they remounted and returned to the Blood village. Bonfires had been lit everywhere, and the entire village was alive with excitement. As Hawk and Two Scalps watched, Black Feather and his warriors rode triumphantly into the village, while behind him on the end of a long reata stumbled the bloody, bedraggled figure of the madman, Elias Hogwood.

When Black Feather arrived at the Gros Ventre camp to find chief Deer Stalker dead and Golden Hawk gone, he had been furious, but not entirely surprised. And when he learned it was the mad trapper, Elias Hogwood, who had betrayed Golden Hawk to the Big Bellies, he decided to go after Hogwood—and forget Golden Hawk for now.

He overtook the trapper sooner than he had thought he would. Hogwood was afoot and had no weapons. From the way he was staggering across the water-less, treeless plain, it was clear he was close to exhaustion. With an exultant cry, Black Feather kicked his pony and charged ahead of his companions.

Once he overtook the dismayed trapper, he cir-cled him, noting with grim satisfaction the mad-man's terrible condition. The side of his skull looked as if it had been furrowed recently with a red-hot iron. And the pure terror in his eyes managed to veil the madness that usually dwelled within them. Black Feather circled him three or four times be-fore lowering his lance and bearing down on him.

Hogwood cried out, turned his back on Black Feather, and began to run. But a pathetic, stum-bling gait was all he could manage as Black Feather kept after him, his lance nudging the trapper's tat-tered backside until at last—completely winded—Hogwood collapsed facedown, too weak to protest as he awaited Black Feather's final blow.

Instead, Black Feather slipped from his pony, unsheathed his knife, and with the tip of it lifted

off the trapper's filthy stocking cap. Flinging it up
to one of his warriors now circling on his pony,
Black Feather reached out and grabbed the trapper's hair. With a deftness born of long practice, he
traced a deep slice in the trapper's scalp and with a
quick snap of his wrist, lifted his trophy, leaving a
hole not much larger than a saucer. Then he stepped
back and held up his trophy for all to see. The
Indians set up a howl and galloped about the two in
celebration.

In a frantic effort to escape, the trapper flung
himself through the grass. But the other warriors
quickly encircled him, forcing him to pull up, cow-
ering, in the grass, while he covered his bleeding
pate with both hands. Reaching his side, Black
Feather had difficulty restraining himself, filled as
he was with such deep contempt for this stinking
piece of offal. Now, sprawled before him in the
grass, he resembled some large, obscene worm. And
this was the same white man who had robbed him
of his furs and then shot him, perfectly content to
let him burn to death in his own campfire.

At that moment a disturbing thought occurred to
Black Feather.

Reaching down, he yanked the trapper around to
face him. As the man flung up his forearm to protect himself, Black Feather struck it angrily away.
"Tell me, Hogwood," he demanded. "Was Golden
Hawk with you when you took my furs?"

Hogwood's eyes lit up. "Yes!" he cried "Yes! It
was all Golden Hawk's idea! He was my partner
last winter. He was the one who told me to take
your furs."

"It was you who pulled me out of my campfire?"

"Yes!"

Stepping back, Black Feather looked down at Hogwood with black disgust. In his craven eagerness to live, Hogwood lied with astonishing stupidity. When Black Feather came awake that night, his clothes still smoking, his chest raw, Hogwood was in the saddle and Golden Hawk was standing by his horse. Golden Hawk had spoken the truth that next morning. Only Black Feather's ungovernable fury had prevented him from accepting it.

Black Feather had wronged a great warrior. Golden Hawk had saved his life.

Black Feather kicked Hogwood in the face. The man's nose disintegrated as he flipped over backward and lay sprawled, unconscious, on the ground before him. Touched by the spirits and gifted with a medicine so fierce and terrible that no warrior dared approach him, Hogwood had long been a scourge to the Blackfoot people. But he was a scourge no longer. His medicine was gone. If he ever had it.

Black Feather turned to the others watching from their ponies. They recognized Hogwood as the mad trapper and were astonished at Black Feather's treatment of him. Seeing this, Black Feather spoke up. "We will take this stinking white trapper back with us and give him to our women. This time he will not escape from the Blackfoot. He has lost his medicine."

"How can that be?" one of the warriors asked anxiously.

"His stench," replied Black Feather. "It has driven away the spirits who lived in him. He is barren now, only a stinking white man. You saw. I took his scalp and no harm befell me."

"The day is not over yet," said another warrior nervously.

"When it is, you will see. Now, do as I say."

One of the warriors dropped the loop of his reata onto the unconscious trapper's chest. Black Feather fitted the rawhide around Hogwood's neck, then tugged it snug. Mounting up, he took the end of the reata and yanked Hogwood to a sitting position. As Hogwood blinked and looked around, blood streaming down his face, Black Feather tugged him onto his feet.

Then Black Feather started back to his village.

The village's frenzied celebration had turned fitful, then guttered out finally like a spent candle. As Hawk and Two Scalps neared Black Feather's tepee, the only thing they could hear was the constant, curiously whooping cries of Elias Hogwood.

They kept on inching through the grass until they were able to see around to the front of Black Feather's lodge. Elias Hogwood was hanging head down from a tripod set up in front of it. Under his head, a low fire was glowing. An old white-haired woman sat dozing beside it, feeding it dry twigs to keep it going at just the right temperature. Hogwood's eyes were blackened holes, his nose two singed orfices. His lips had peeled back from the heat, revealing his blackened, irregular teeth. All the hair had been burnt off his head and his roasted scalp had split away from his skull as it shrunk, pieces of it hanging down into the fire, its blackened strips smoking.

Hogwood's brains were frying, but he was not dead. His constant, mewling cries—no longer seeming to come from anything human—filled the dark, moonless night like some insane lullaby. Hogwood had been stripped naked, and when Hawk looked more closely and saw around which portion of Hogwood's anatomy the rawhide holding him had been tied, he groaned inwardly.

Hawk glanced at Two Scalps and pointed to the old woman. He nodded, left Hawk, and a moment later came at her from behind. Clamping a hand about her mouth, he bent her head back, then lifted her. Her spine snapped like a dead branch, but Hawk paid no heed as he darted out and, with one slash of his knife, cut Hogwood down. Dragging the trapper into the shadows behind Black Feather's lodge, Hawk leaned his mouth close to what was left of the man's ears.

"It's me, Hogwood!" he told him. "Hawk!"

The man had stopped mewling the moment Hawk grabbed him. Now, in words that seemed to be coming from the bottom of a fathomless well, he gasped, *"Kill me!"*

"First, you bastard—where's my Hawken rifle," Hawk demanded. "Has Black Feather got it?"

Hogwood's blackened mouth seemed to change its shape, to smile almost as he stared blindly up at

Hawk. "Two Comanche ..." Hogwood gasped. "They took it. Your cabin ... waiting ... you ... !"

Hawk leaned closer to Hogwood. "What're you sayin'?" he demanded in a fierce whisper. "What Comanches?"

But Hawk got no answer—only a soft rattle—or was it a chuckle? Then came the same plea as before, uttered from deep within the man's tormented soul: *"Kill me! Please!"*

Hawk sat back on his haunches and gazed bitterly down at Hogwood. Even naked with his head and shoulders roasted, the trapper still stank like a skunk in heat. Hawk glanced questioningly at Two Scalps, who had just come up beside him. The Flathead shrugged and looked with little interest at the skull-like face.

Again there came that terrible, gasping plea. This time Hawk heeded it. Lifting his knife, he plunged it down through the man's heart. Hogwood seemed to tremble along his entire length. Hawk made sure he was dead with another swift downward plunge of his knife. Then he calmly wiped the blade clean on the grass.

Hawk's emotions were mixed. He hated Hogwood, and if he had let him live, the Blackfoot would have been able to drag out his miserable death for two, possibly three more days. So Hawk had just done the sonofabitch a great favor.

But what had the trapper already done to him?

Two Comanches had his Hawken. Once again, it seemed, he was being stalked by his old tribesmen, their thirst for glory demanding they make this deadly quest. And there was something about his cabin as well. The only thing it could mean was that Hogwood had given his rifle to these Comanche and then directed them to Hawk's cabin on the Snake. Groaning inwardly, Hawk thought of Raven Eyes then and prayed she was still with her sister's people. He thought of Angus too, recalling his request that he stop off at the cabin to tell Raven Eyes—if she were there—that he would soon be back. Hawk could only hope that Angus would not be so unlucky as to reach his cabin when those two Comanche did.

Hawk looked back down at Hogwood. Perhaps he should not have killed him after all. He should have let the bastard roast a few more days.

Two Scalps was already moving off. Turning, Hawk saw him snaking silently through the grass toward the rear of Black Feather's lodge. Hawk joined him. Two Scalps slit a hole in the hide covering the lodge and the two men slipped through it and found themselves only a few feet from Black Feather. He was on his back, his mouth partly open, snoring softly.

The two men had long since rehearsed what they would do.

After a glance over at Black Feather's woman to make sure she was asleep, Two Scalps clapped one hand over the warrior's mouth to prevent an outcry, while Hawk lifted the war club Two Scalps had given him and brought it down with stunning force onto Black Feather's head, knocking the warrior senseless. Then the two men dragged Black Feather silently out of the lodge. Once outside, Two Scalps draped Black Feather over his shoul-

ders and the two men splashed across the stream
and disappeared into the darkness under the ravine's rim.

Gazing down at the shattered wagons and the
dim burial mounds of so many people Hawk had
known sent a cold shudder down his spine. He
looked back at the tightly bound Blood chief responsible and pointed. Black Feather's mouth was
a grim line, and though he followed Hawk's pointing finger, he said nothing at all, made no comment,
indicated no remorse.

Hawk understood. It was all in the nature of
things for this Blood chief to kill whites and Flatheads, all those who did not serve the interests of
his people or who threatened their way of life.
Hawk looked beyond Black Feather at Two Scalps.

The Flathead warrior nodded grimly and stepped
closer to the captured chief. Like Hawk, Two Scalps
was eager to finish what had to be done, then move
on. During the long ride to this place, they had only
just managed to elude Blood war parties trying to
overtake them. At that very moment, as both men
knew for certain, a large Blood war party was less
than a mile from them. They did not have much
more time.

Hawk had already done much thinking on the
matter. Since the graves below them were meant to
serve as a warning to any who might attempt to
cross Blackfoot land, it would be only fitting, Hawk
felt, that Black Feather's rotting corpse should hang
over the gorge as a warning to all Blackfoot who might
wish to treat settlers in such a summary manner.

The three were standing on a finger of rock projecting out over the gorge. Anchored to the ledge was a lone pine, its convoluted branches clasping it like the fingers of an ancient hand. One branch of this pine hung out over the gorge. Black Feather's corpse would be hung from this branch.

Hawk looked into Black Feather's obsidian eyes. He and Two Scalps had not yet decided which of them was to take the Blood chief's scalp, but it would be taken. Of that there could be no doubt. Still, Hawk found himself unwilling to kill Black Feather while his hands were trussed behind him.

"Untie him," Hawk told Two Scalps.

Two Scalps looked at Hawk, as if to say, "What is the matter, white man? Are you going soft?" Then, with a shrug, he sliced through the rawhide binding Black Feather's ankles, then cut away those binding his wrists. He stepped back then, his knife still in his hand, as Black Feather rubbed his hands together to regain his circulation.

"All right, Two Scalps," Hawk said, coming to his decision suddenly. "He's yours. Take his scalp if you want."

But before Two Scalps could step forward to take his trophy, Black Feather swung around suddenly, snatched the pistol from Two Scalps' belt, and then backed swiftly away from both of them, the pistol leveled at Hawk.

"You would let this Flathead take my scalp?" he asked Hawk.

"Yes."

"Why? Does the great Golden Hawk not feel Black Feather's scalp is a worthy trophy for such as him."

"I have enough trophies, Black Feather."

Black Feather pointed the gun at Hawk's chest, his finger tightening about the trigger, his eyes cold with resolve. His knife out, Hawk took a step forward, determined to die hard as he prepared himself for the crash of the revolver, the stunning impact of the round. Abruptly, the resolve in Black Feather's eyes wavered and, inexplicably, the warrior turned his back on Hawk and fired on Two Scalps.

Hawk drew his knife and fell on Black Feather, chopping his blade down swiftly—again and again until he had lost count. Under the storm of knife strokes, Black Feather collapsed to the ground. Stepping away from the chieftain's bloody torso, Hawk looked over at Two Scalps. His Flathead companion had taken the ball in the chest, directly over his heart, and was already a dead man.

Hawk glanced down at Black Feather. His heart was still pounding, his mind swarming with questions. Why had Black Feather fired on Two Scalps and not him? Why in that last minute, had his resolve wavered, causing him to turn his back on Hawk and on Hawk's knife.

Black Feather stirred. Hawk went down on one knee beside him. The warrior opened his eyes and looked up at Hawk. For a fleeting moment a smile of grim satisfaction lighted his face.

"Why didn't you pull that trigger, Black Feather?" Hawk demanded. "You been after me for a long time."

"I speak to mad trapper, the stinking one. He lie, and I see the truth."

"The truth?"

"You say once you are not my enemy. It is true. You pull me from the fire. You save my life. I pay debt. Take now my life in exchange for yours."

Before Hawk could make any kind of response, Black Feather's head fell back, his eyes remaining open to the sky. Hawk closed them both, then stood up. He was confused—and saddened—not only at the death of Two Scalps, but at the death of this terrible and implacable warrior, a brave man for all of that—and one who paid his debts.

Hawk did not feel it would serve any sane purpose for the Blood warrior's body to hang as a warning above the gorge, food for buzzards until his bones were picked clean. Instead, he buried him on a small rise alongside his foe, Two Scalps, the two warriors asleep in a common sepulcher, enemies no longer.

Then he set his face south.

If he had heard Hogwood right, once again—as inevitable as flies in springtime—Comanche warriors were waiting for him.

—— Chapter Ten ——

When Hawk reached Fort Union a week later, he found from talking to a couple of mountain men that Angus MacDougal—moving around more easily on new boots he traded for—had already been there and left. Joe Meek, Hawk was advised, had gone off also, this time, according to his own words, to find himself a quiet stream where he could set down his traps and get away from the smell of wagon grease and the cries of snot-nosed children.

Ken Mackenzie, the builder and chief factor of Fort Union, approached Hawk a few hours after his arrival and invited him to his quarters atop the blockhouse for supper and a smoke. As soon as his Indian housekeeper brought out the afterdinner brandy and the Mexican cheroots, Mackenzie, dressed in his usual ruffled silk shirt, lit up his cheroot and made clear his reason for inviting Hawk to supper.

"When you rode in this afternoon, Hawk, I noticed you weren't pushing that Indian pony of yours very hard. Any reason for that?"

"Why should I be pushing it?"

"You mean you didn't know?"

"Know what?"

"Who was following you?"

"Oh. You mean the Blackfoot."

"Them's who I meant, all right. Didn't you know they were on your tail?"

"Sure, I knew. But I had plenty of time, I figured."

"Well, maybe this time you figured wrong."

Mackenzie opened the doors leading out onto his balcony which was connected to a narrow catwalk that ran along the top of the fort's log palisades. Mackenzie beckoned Hawk to follow. Stepping out onto the balcony, they walked to the railing, where Mackenzie pointed to a meadow on the other side of the Missouri. Along the river's embankment a long line of lodges had been set up. Blackfoot lodges. Hawk counted ten in all.

"How long they been there?" he asked.

"Since an hour after you arrived."

"I must be slipping. I thought they were only a few minutes behind me."

"Dammit, Hawk. You know the trouble we've been having with them devils. The company has had to abandon two trading posts because of them. And now here we've got more of them to worry about, thanks to you. This spring two of our men were killed and a dozen horses driven off."

"I heard all about it from Joe Meek. Hell, Mac, why blame me? Chardon's the one at fault. Him and his crazy temper."

"I admit it, Hawk. But that don't make the ar-

rival of these new Blood warriors any more com-
forting."

Hawk shrugged and gazed at the distant lodges.
The trader Hawk referred to was François Chardon,
who this past winter fired a cannon into a Piegan
band who had come to trade at Fort Union. Chardon
and his partner, it appeared, had become incensed
when some Blackfoot had stolen a pig from them
earlier.

"If I brought you trouble, Mac, I'm sorry."

"What the hell happened? You kill a chief, or
something?"

Hawk told him about the wagon train—not the
entire story, but enough for Mackenzie to understand what Hawk had been up to. He was a sober
man when Hawk finished his tale.

"What the hell, Mac," Hawk said, finishing his
brandy. "Black Feather's Blood band never did trade
much with this fort, anyway. What did you lose?"

"His ain't the only Blood band out there. I was
thinking of sending Jacob Berger back into the
Blackfoot country. I figured if he could smoke awhile
with Iron Shirt, things might get back to normal.
I'll take all the buffalo pelts they can get for me—
and you know Hudson's Bay won't touch a one."

"Hell, Mac, relax. Don't be so impatient. Wait
awhile. This'll blow over. You can send Berger in
later, before the snow flies."

Mackenzie's face went cold with resolve. "Hawk,
I can send him a good deal sooner if you'll leave
this fort as soon as you can. That way I won't have
to explain to them devils over there why I'm pro-

tecting Golden Hawk, the white man who killed one of their chiefs."

"You mean you're sidin' with them?"

"I mean I'm here to trade with them, Hawk. Do you understand? Trade with them. But I can't do that if everyone's killing everyone else."

"I'll pull out tomorrow then, first thing. But I'll need some fresh horses and a rifle."

"What happened to your Hawken?"

"That crazy son-of-a-bitch Hogwood stole it. He said two Comanche took it from him. But I find that hard to believe."

"Did you say Hogwood? You mean that crazy no-account is still out there?"

"Not anymore."

Mackenzie looked warily at Hawk, then sighed. "All right, Hawk. Don't tell me anymore. Just leave this place. And if it'll help you get out of here any sooner, I'll supply you with whatever you need."

Hawk tossed the stump of his cheroot off the balcony. "That suits me fine, Mac," he said. "Come on back inside, and I'll give you a list."

With a curt nod, Mackenzie turned and led Hawk back off the balcony.

Leading a big chestnut, a flintlock rifle altered for percussion in his sling and a serviceable Paterson Colt in his belt, Hawk slipped out of the fort a little after midnight, left the Missouri River and the fort behind, and headed south along the Yellowstone. Once he was clear of the fort, he mounted up and lifted the horse to a lope.

He had not gone far when he realized he had not

left all his Blackfoot pursuers behind. Slipping off his mount, he pulled it after him into a patch of willows in the river's shallows and waited. Before long a file of six mounted Blackfoot passed in the darkness. His hand over the chestnut's snout, Hawk waited until they were well gone, then rode into the river, gave the chestnut its head, and let it carry him across. Gaining the timber on the other side, Hawk cut directly west, intending to cross the mountains above Pierre's Hole, then swing south to his cabin.

The two Comanche who had taken Golden Hawk's rifle from Hogwood were called Little Dog and Returns-to-Battle. They were members of the Nokoni band, one which lived far from those Comanche who had taken the young Golden Hawk and his sister into their band.

Nevertheless, every Nokoni warrior knew of Golden Hawk's treachery while he was a member of the Kwahadi band and of the awesome toll he had taken on those Kwahadi braves who had journeyed north since to find and punish him. Indeed, since the moment Little Dog and Returns-to-Battle first heard the old ones chanting of Golden Hawk deeds around their fires, they knew the day would come when they too made the journey north to join in combat with Golden Hawk. That so many had vanished in this quest only filled them with an unquenchable desire to follow after them. Their only prayer was that no one would kill Golden Hawk before they reached him.

The Indian with the limp was Returns-to-Battle.

He had lost his horse while fighting Apaches and had walked calmly back into the thundering melee and killed three Apaches before a horse trampled him, breaking his leg. Despite the broken leg, he had ridden back the two hundred miles to his village without a single outcry. After all that punishment, the leg had never properly healed.

But Returns-to-Battle's bravery and fortitude had won him the chief's woman he sought and now he served as the leader of this quest. Little Dog, his friend and fellow comrade in arms, willingly followed his lead. The two had fought side by side many times, and in the midst of some battles they had bound their ankles together, vowing not to leave the other until the battle was done.

When that evil-smelling trapper told them Golden Hawk had been killed by the Blackfoot, their dismay had been genuine. Though they had not entirely believed it when the trapper changed his story and told them that Golden Hawk had gone south to his cabin on the Snake, it was all they had to go on—that and a desperate hope that Golden Hawk still lived. And now this hope had blossomed into a near certainty by their discovery in Fort Hall a few days ago of a redheaded trapper who spoke openly of his friendship with Golden Hawk.

The white man had no toes, but he walked well enough in boots stuffed with cloth. Still, he remained in the saddle for the most part, even when he was only crossing from one side of the fort to the other. The two Comanche made use of an old Crow Indian who lived in his ragged lodge outside the fort. They supplied him with rum and in gratitude he told them all he could about those who frequented this fort. Thus was he able to tell them that this strange white man without toes had recently mentioned that he would soon leave the fort to journey to the cabin of Golden Hawk.

Now, standing in the morning mists surrounding Fort Hall, the two Comanche watched the white trapper ride out of the fort, his packhorse following behind him. He was wearing a wide-brimmed hat over his long, stringy red hair, a sleeveless jacket fashioned from buffalo hide, buckskin leggings, and shiny black boots. They waited until he was out of sight, then mounted up and followed him, careful to keep well back. His spoor would be easy enough to follow, since Returns-to-Battle had cut a notch in the hoof on the trapper's packhorse's right front foreleg.

The rum-soaked Crow had no honor. Only an enormous thirst. Perfectly willing to keep the two Comanche informed of all who came to and went from Fort Hall, for an equal supply of rum he had also kept Angus MacDougal apprised of the two Comanche, especially their keen interest in him and in the whereabouts of Hawk's cabin.

Keeping to a southerly course—the opposite direction from Hawk's cabin—Angus kept on through rough country for two days, until he found himself moving through a ravine. A swift stream cut the center of it, and Angus followed a narrow game trail high above. He soon realized he had found the place where he could rid himself of his Comanche pursuers.

Dismounting near dusk, he tethered his horses in a small glen below the trail and close to the water, then made a dry camp on the slope above. After midnight he bunched up his blanket to make it look as if he were still sleeping under it, then moved awkwardly down the slope to his horse, saddled it and rode back along the trail until he came upon the two Comanche ponies, tethered in a small grassy area close under a rocky outcropping. Remaining on his horse, he leaned over and cut the rawhide holding them, after which he led the ponies behind him farther down the trail. Once far enough from where he'd found them, he slapped them on the rump and sent them on a gallop deeper into the ravine. Then he rode back to where they had been tethered.

Dismounting, he stumbled further on until he caught sight of the Comanche's sleeping forms. They were close by the edge of the ravine. Embers from their campfire still glowed beside them, which told Angus the two had as yet no idea he was on to them. He looked over the campsite. He was pleased. It could not have been more perfect for his purposes, he realized.

He groped clumsily back to his horse, mounted up, and rode back a little ways, then dismounted to wait for just a little more light. To take out the two of them, he had long since realized, he would have to do more than open fire on them. He was not that sure of his marksmanship, and if one of them escaped his first volley, Angus would have a hell of a time finishing him off, hampered as he was by these toeless feet of his.

But on horseback it would be an entirely different matter.

For a while after the sun came up, mists from the stream below the trail filled the ravine. Angus, already mounted and screened by a fir tree, waited impatiently for the mists to clear off the trail ahead. When it did, he saw that the two Indians were already awake. One was sitting up, the other was standing in front of him, pissing off the trail into the stream below. They were talking, but were too far away for Angus to make out a word, even if he could understand Comanche.

His rifle was primed and ready, the round seated securely, the charge sufficient to send the ball clean through the nearest one. His charging horse could take care of the other. Holding the rifle in his right hand, Angus spurred his horse to a sudden gallop and bore down on the two Indians.

Both were on their feet when he swept into view. Bending low over his horse's neck, Angus lifted his rifle and fired. The round caught the nearest one full in the chest. The other one, his dick no longer in his hand, tried to swing up a rifle a second before Angus's horse slammed into him. The Comanche catapulted off the trail and went spinning into the stream below. Wheeling, Angus galloped back and peered down at the stream in time to see what he presumed was the Comanche's body being slammed past a boulder. A moment later the Comanche had been swept out of sight.

Angus dismounted. Holding on to his mount's halter to steady himself, he approached the Comanche he had shot. This was not the one with the gimpy leg. He was a young brave, and the look on his face was one of pure surprise. Shaking his head at the waste of it, Angus wondered why in hell this fool Indian and his buddy were hunting Golden Hawk's scalp this far from home.

Glancing down into the gorge, he saw the rifle the other comanche had tried to use lying in the rocks where it had fallen. Angus did not see how he could get himself down there to retrieve it—not without getting himself very wet.

With a shrug, he mounted up and rode back down the trail to retrieve his packhorse and the rest of his gear. He was a lot farther from Hawk's cabin that he had been when he left the fort, but that didn't matter. After all, there was no certainty that after this much time Hawk's woman would still be there waiting for him to come back. And if she wasn't there, why he'd just make himself comfortable in the cabin awhile. He had had one very busy summer and needed to rest up. Yes sir, one that had seen him break free at last from his Gros Ventre captors—not to mention that she-devil of a wife. He wouldn't even miss the young hellions he'd sired.

He would never be able to thank Golden Hawk enough.

Returns-to-Battle was not able to pull himself out of the swift water until he had been swept at least a quarter of a mile farther into the gorge. When he did succeed in pulling himself onto the bank, he found his right ankle was swollen to nearly twice its size. He must have come down awkwardly on it when he hit the rocks at the stream's edge. He sat awhile contemplating his miserable luck, aware of the ankle's growing, throbbing ache. He stared at it ruefully, then decided he had no choice but to treat this with the contempt it deserved, and forced himself to sit up and climb back up onto the trail, his ankle protesting each move he made, it seemed.

He had not gone far when he found his and Little Dog's ponies cropping grass beside the trail. He struggled onto his pony and drove the other one ahead of him, and before long was back at their campsite. The white eyes had not disturbed any of their gear and had ridden off leaving Little Dog where he had fallen.

With a deep, unhappy sigh, Returns-to-Battle dismounted and saw to the burial rites of his dead comrade. Afterward, he checked under his blanket and found that the Walker Colt he had taken from the Stinking One was still there. Glancing down into the gorge, he saw Golden Hawk's rifle resting among the rocks. Doing his best to ignore the sharp pain in his ankle, he managed to work himself down to the rocks and back up again with the rifle. He found a chip in the rifle's stock, but otherwise it was in fine condition.

An hour later he was mounted up and on his way again, still following the redheaded trapper. He was confident that the fool would now head straight for the cabin and Golden Hawk. At the same time he was aware that he might have broken—not sprained—his ankle. When the time came for him to do battle with Golden Hawk, this injury would hamper him greatly.

But he would deal with that when the time came.

* * *

All during the stranger's long ride up the slope, Raven Eyes kept her rifle trained on him. She kept out of sight, however, peering through one of the front windows. The rider was wearing a black, wide-brimmed hat and a vest made from buffalo hide. As his horse brought him closer, he leaned forward in his saddle to peer anxiously at the cabin. It was clear he had seen the smoke from her chimney and was expecting someone to step out and greet him.

She had had no trouble yet from the trappers in this region. They all knew she was Hawk's woman, though some—like herself at times—wondered openly when he was going to show up again, obviously hoping she would tire of the wait. But this trapper she had never seen before. Where had he come from? she wondered.

Abruptly, less than fifty feet from the cabin's door, he pulled his horse to a halt and cupped his hand around his mouth.

"Hello, anyone in the cabin!" he called.

She hesitated a moment longer, then stepped out through the doorway, her rifle cradled in her arm. "Who are you?" she spoke in passable English. "What you want?"

He smiled, his china-blue eyes glowing with relief. "Found you, did I?" he exclaimed. "Are you Raven Eyes?"

"I am Raven Eyes."

"You Golden Hawk's woman?"

"Yes."

"Well, I got news for you then."

"I listen."

"I left him not too long ago. He says to hang in there, he'll be back shortly."

Raven Eyes was overjoyed. She could hardly believe her ears. "You see him? Where?"

"Last time was in Blackfoot country. He was going after a mean one, Black Feather."

"Then he back from East where he visited his sister?" asked Raven Eyes.

"He's back all right." The trapper peered at her and at the rifle she was still packing. "You goin' to let me in? I'm plumb wore out."

She quickly lowered the rifle and stepped aside. "Yes. Yes. Come inside. I will make coffee."

Grinning with pleasure, the trapper came toward her, walking with a curiously upright gait, as if he did not dare lean forward. Doffing his hat as he passed her, he entered the cabin.

She hurried in after him to put the coffee on, her heart thudding with excitement, so anxious was she to hear what this stranger had to tell her. But he had already told her the most important thing.

As Golden Hawk had promised her, he had come back.

—— Chapter Eleven ——

Protecting his ankle as well as he could, Returns-to-Battle dropped from his horse. He now realized it was broken. With each passing moment the pain increased relentlessly. Landing in a patch of deep grass, he allowed himself to rest for a few minutes before lifting his head to peer up the slope at the cabin.

Using the Hawken rifle for support, he pushed himself upright, then slapped his pony on its rump, sending it deeper into the timber. Leaning back against a tree, he dropped his last three cartridges into the Walker Colt's cylinders, then loaded the rifle. Using the rifle's stock for support, he moved painfully up through the timber toward the cabin sitting on the ridge's crest. Keeping upright on the treacherous pine needles was not easy. No matter how carefully he put down the rifle's butt, his foot occasionally brushed the ground, sending an almost paralyzing bolt of pain up his leg and deep into his groin.

As he struggled on through the timber, thoughts

of Little Dog intruded on his concentration. At times his grief threatened to overwhelm him. Though Little Dog's death made him more fiercely determined than ever to take Golden Hawk's scalp, he had no illusions as to what lay ahead of him. Despite his present condition he would most surely kill Golden Hawk and the redheaded trapper. But taking Golden Hawk's scalp all the way back to his village might not be possible.

Still, he had not come this far to fail now.

For one thing, everything that foul-smelling white man told them had been true. At the fort he and Little Dog had heard of Golden Hawk's woman, and just as the groveling white man had told them, her name was Raven Eyes. The redheaded trapper would not have attacked them if he had not been fearful they were trailing him to Golden Hawk's cabin. And now he had led Returns-to-Battle to it. Golden Hawk must be inside at that very moment, greeting the redheaded one.

Approaching the timber's edge finally, he peered through the trees at the cabin. The trapper had left his horses in front of it. Smoke lifted from the chimney. He could smell coffee. As he stood leaning against a tree, the redheaded trapper pushed through the door to tend to his horses. Returns-to-Battle kept perfectly still as he watched the trapper lead the horses to the small barn alongside the cabin. It was close to dusk. Returns-to-Battle decided he would wait until the trapper rejoined Golden Hawk inside the cabin before making his move.

Surprise, he realized, was all he had going for

him. But this could be everything. At sight of Little
Dog's killer, his eagerness for battle had redoubled,
and he felt now the spiritual presence of Little Dog
waiting eagerly beside him.

It was dark. A weary Angus MacDougal, his stomach pleasantly distended from his recent meal,
snored on a cot in the far corner. Raven Eyes,
humming softly to herself, was in the act of clearing off the table, dropping the dishes into her wooden
bucket as she circled it. She was thinking of Golden
Hawk with an aching heart. Angus had told her
why he had not returned with him to the cabin,
and she accepted Hawk's need to go after this filthy
Blackfoot war chief. But even though he was the
mighty warrior he was, she could not help but
worry.

The door swung wide—or rather it was pounded
open by the stock of a rifle. Turning, Raven Eyes
saw a Comanche warrior leaning on the doorjamb, a
huge Walker Colt in one hand, Golden Hawk's rifle
in the other.

Angus jumped up, fully awake in an instant. Raven Eyes heard his muffled curse as the Comanche
swung the Colt toward Angus and fired. The round
slammed into the trapper, but she was only dimly
aware of this as she flung herself at the Indian, the
bucket held over her head. The Comanche turned
back to her as she brought the bucket down upon
him. His big Colt detonated. The slug slammed into
the bucket, knocking it from her hands.

By then she had reached the Indian. Her fingers
clawed for his throat. He flung her aside, then

swiped viciously at her with the barrel of his Colt. The blow knocked her nearly senseless. She staggered out of the cabin and collapsed to the ground.

Behind her she heard dimly the sounds of a struggle within the cabin as the wounded Angus fought with the Comanche. The Colt detonated again. She heard Angus's terrible cry. It galvanized her and she crawled off toward the barn. . . .

From the moment Hawk lifted into the mountains above Pierre's Hole, he felt better. The pines filled the high, clean air with an intoxicating perfume. Birds sang. He could hear the movement of small animals in the brush about him. Rabbits, woodchucks, and one or two foxes scurried off at his approach and through the files of timber, he glimpsed the flashing tails of bounding deer.

When he rode finally into the foothills only a few miles from his cabin, he began recognizing familiar landmarks—a granite cliff face in the distance, a lone, lightning-blasted pine on a ridge far to his right. Other landmarks loomed up about him like familiar faces, and his heart raced with eagerness as he thought of the cozy warmth of his cabin— and Raven Eyes.

Of course it was more than likely she was still with her sister's people, but there was always the chance she might have returned to the cabin to wait for him. He felt a tinge of guilt for not having returned earlier; and when he thought of Melanie and all the others in that wagon train, and recalled the crazed Elias Hogwood and that fierce Blackfoot chief he had saved only to kill—it seemed as if he were waking at last from a hellish nightmare.

So far he had seen no sign of the two Comanche Hogwood had mentioned. But at the moment he spoke, Hogwood had been nearly out of his mind with pain and terror. How could Hawk credit the ravings of anyone in that condition? Even under normal circumstances, Hogwood was a liar and a blackguard. And even if Hogwood *had* told any Comanche of his cabin—how in hell would they ever find it in these mountains?

Dusk fell swiftly, then darkness. Hawk was less than a day's journey from the cabin. He made camp certain he would arrive there by noon the next day. Perhaps on his way he would bring down a buck. If Angus was waiting for him at the cabin, the two men would have a feast.

The prospect so pleased him that after he pulled his blanket over his shoulder and closed his eyes, he fell immediately asleep.

Hawk pulled up. During the morning's ride, he had not been able to bring down a buck, but he had managed to shoot two grouse, and these now hung from his cantle. Despite the promise of a good meal, however, he glanced about him, vaguely troubled— his enormous delight at reaching the cabin giving way to a dim sense of foreboding. It was a past noon, yet no smoke coiled from the cabin's chimney. This in itself was nothing. Angus was not necessarily waiting there. He could be anywhere in these mountains, trapping or finding his own place. But what bothered Hawk was the brooding silence that hung over the meadow and the ridge above.

He dismounted, slipped his rifle from its sling, and darted over into the timber, then moved swiftly up the slope to the ridge, keeping in the woods until he was close to the cabin. The door hung open. He told himself this did not have to mean trouble. With Raven Eyes away at her people's village, squatters or mountain men could have used the cabin, not being too careful about how they left it.

But even as Hawk told himself this, he knew he was whistling past the graveyard.

The faint, unmistakable scent of woodsmoke hung in the air, which meant the cabin's fireplace had been used as recently as the previous day—more likely the night before. And then from the small barn he heard the sound of impatient horses stamping in their stalls. Fighting back a growing sense of alarm, Hawk broke from the timber and ran across the yard. Reaching the cabin, he pulled up— amazed—at sight of his Walker Colt lying in the grass in front of the open door.

He charged into the cabin, then pulled up at once, a groan issuing from deep within him.

Angus MacDougal had reached the cabin ahead of him, all right. And he was still here. His red hair now a gory crown, the Scotsman hung from a rafter, naked, bloody strips of skin hanging from his fly-covered torso. Hogwood had not been out of his head, after all. Those two Comanche *had* found his cabin. The miserable reach of that trapper seemed infinite. From the moment Hawk came upon Hogwood, he had known only trouble—and death.

Hawk cut Angus down. Wrapping him in a blanket, he dragged the body outside. Glimpsing the man's pitiful toeless feet, the raw strips of flesh hanging from his ravaged torso, his open, gaping mouth—as if he were still screaming out in pain—Hawk felt his stomach twist in dismay and grief. Bending close, he closed Angus's wide-open, staring eyes and did his best to wave off the persistent flies.

Digging a shallow grave on a rise behind the cabin, Hawk lowered his old friend into his final resting place and then drove a crude cross into the ground with the blade of his shovel. Afterward, for a long, painful moment, he bent his head and prayed over Angus, his heart raging. Angus had gone through so much during a hateful captivity, then had made his move and escaped back into the world, a free man once more—only to have it end like this.

Hawk hurried back toward the cabin. Snatching up his Walker Colt, he did not fail to wonder at the grim fate that had returned it to him. Then he entered the cabin and searched for any sign that Raven Eyes might have been there with Angus. His hope was that, as he had half expected, she had indeed remained with her people—that Angus had been alone in the cabin when the Comanche burst in on him.

Glancing over at the table still upright in one corner, he saw only a single dinner plate and place setting. For a moment this satisfied him that Angus had been alone. Then he caught sight of a water bucket in the corner. It was on its side, a bullet hole punched through it. Picking it up, he looked inside. Knives and forks, cups, a platter and another dinner plate rested in it. The plate had been shattered by the bullet that had slammed through the bucket's wooden side. Again Hawk glanced over at the table. A lone spoon sat across from the remaining plate. The broken plate inside this bucket had come from that place setting.

In that instant Hawk knew what must have happened the night before.

Raven Eyes had been clearing off the table. As was her custom, she had been circling it—dropping the dishes into the water bucket—when the Comanche stormed through the door. Angus must have gone for his gun and perhaps she had thrown the bucket at one of the Comanche. Groaning inwardly, Hawk visualized Raven Eyes in the midst of the sudden cross fire.

But there was no sign of her, and this gave him a desperate hope. She could have fled. She might still be alive.

Rushing from the cabin, he hurried into the barn to see if she had hidden herself there. He passed the stalls where Angus's mount and packhorse, out of water and feed, still stamped restlessly. In the stall next to them, he saw the fresh hoofprints of Raven Eyes' pony as they bit through the straw. They led from the barn and headed across the meadow toward the timber. He went back for his horse, checked the load on his rifle, and rode across the meadow.

Just inside the timber, he found Raven Eyes'

dead pony. It had been felled from behind by a single bullet, then left to thrash itself to death. Beyond the dead pony, Hawk caught the faint imprint of Raven Eyes' moccasins and the untidy prints of what he now realized was only a single Comanche warrior in pursuit of her. Deeper into the timber, her spoor and that of the Comanche pursuing her vanished as they traveled across pine-carpeted ground. Hawk kept on nevertheless and broke out onto a familiar high meadow, where he again caught sight of Raven Eyes' moccasin prints. She was heading straight for a towering pile of rocks bordering the meadow's far side. Hawk caught another sign as well—something stranger than footprints and much less easy to understand.

It was as if a giant snake of some kind were pulling itself through the grass after Raven Eyes.

He spurred across the meadow, heading for the rocks, the pound of his mount's hooves muffled by the deep grass. Reaching the rocks, he reined in to look up at them, certain by now that Raven Eyes had taken refuge somewhere among them. Without warning, a Comanche dragged himself into view on top of a flat boulder, Hawk's own rifle at his shoulder. Before the Comanche could pull the trigger, however, a maddened Raven Eyes flung herself from a rock ledge just above him, crashing down upon the Comanche a second before the rifle detonated. The bullet plowed into the ground before Hawk as Raven Eyes, by this time a maddened she-devil, scratched and kicked the Comanche, sending them both tumbling off the boulder to the thick grass below.

Hawk leaped to the ground, and pulled the furious Raven Eyes off the Comanche. Glaring balefully up at Hawk, the Comanche warrior leaned defiantly back on his elbows, and Hawk saw his purple, distended ankle. It was almost certainly broken, and then he understood the long, sinuous trail he had found through the grass. Aiming his rifle down at the Comanche, Hawk's finger tightened on the trigger—but he did not pull it.

"What band are you from?" he demanded.

In a curiously southern drawl, the Comanche replied, "The Nokoni band."

"Where is the other one, your comrade?"

"On way here old redhead trapper kill him." The Comanche smiled coldly then. "I make him think on this for a long time before I let him die. So now you make me suffer too."

Hawk did not reply. For a while back there, he had been afraid that when it came to dealing with these savages, he was losing his edge. Well, he wasn't. He couldn't afford to do that. Ever.

If Hawk were to let this Comanche go free, he would only return—with a stump for a foot, no doubt—and once again do his best to kill Hawk. Like all his kind, this Comanche was implacable. Hawk could expect nothing less from these fierce warriors. They were what they were: warriors of the Stone Age. It was as pure and simple as that. As an eagle had talons and a grizzly claws, so the Comanche and the rest of their savage legions knew no mercy.

And expected none.

Hawk stepped back, took careful aim—and fired

into the Comanche's heart. As the Indian slammed back into the grass, Hawk turned to Raven Eyes.

She was on her feet now, bedraggled and weary, bits of straw still clinging to her long black tresses. He opened his arms and she rushed into them, her wild heart throbbing against his.

He held her for a long, delicious moment, then stepped back to smile down at her. "You just saved my life."

"Yes."

"And if I hadn't pulled you off that Comanche, I think you would have scratched his eyes out."

"I am sorry you did not let me."

"You are a savage woman."

She smiled. "And you are Golden Hawk."

"That's right," he replied, lifting her onto his horse

Leaving the dead Comanche for the wolves, Hawk mounted up behind Raven Eyes, turned the horse, and rode back across the meadow.

As he rode, he could see beyond the timber to the distant, snowcapped mountains. In order to fill the winter's larder, Raven Eyes and he would soon be hunting for deer and elk on those timbered slopes. The smell of snow was already in the air. At this height, the first snow would fall soon. And with it would come bright days with snow-blanketed meadows brilliant in the sun—and long winter nights alone with Raven Eyes.

He could no longer recall clearly those towns through which he had traveled during his journey east. Their stench and swarming streets were fading from his memory like the shards of a bad dream.

But if his sister Annabelle was happy, that was all that mattered. And now he was home again. Still holding the reins, he tightened his arms about Raven Eyes' slim waist.

In response, she learned her back against him. He caught the intoxicating scent of her luxuriant hair. If in Melanie's embrace he had ever doubted it, he did so no longer. He was content. This was his land and Raven Eyes was his woman. The same savage heart that beat in all her kinsmen throbbed in her bosom as well.

And this night it would throb in unison with his.

ROY HOGAN KEEPS THE WEST WILD

☐ **THE DOOMSDAY MARSHAL AND THE HANGING JUDGE by Ray Hogan.** John Rye had only his two guns to protect the most hated man in the west. That's why he was picked to ride gun for the judge who strung up more men than any other judge. It's a twisting terror trail for Rye—from Arizona to Nebraska. (151410—$2.75)

☐ **THE RAWHIDERS.** Forced outside the law, Matt Buckman had to shoot his way back in. Rescued from the savage Kiowas by four men who appeared suddenly to save him, Matt Buckman felt responsible for the death of one and vowed to ride in his place. Soon he discovered that filling the dead man's boots would not be easy . . . he was riding with a crew of killers . . . killers he owed his life to. . . . (143922—$2.75)

☐ **THE MAN WHO KILLED THE MARSHAL.** He had to force justice from the law—at gunpoint. Dan Reneger had come to the settlement at the edge of nowhere to escape his gunslinging past. But he was in trouble from the start . . . in a town where the marshal knew his name.
(148193—$2.50)

☐ **THE HELL ROAD.** He was carrying a treacherous hostage and a million dollar coffin through a death trap! He was fair game for Indians, Confederates and bandits, but Marshak was the only man in the Union who could handle this impossible mission—all he had to do was survive. (147863—$2.50)

Prices slightly higher in Canada.

Buy them at your local bookstore or use this convenient coupon for ordering.

NEW AMERICAN LIBRARY,
P.O. Box 999, Bergenfield, New Jersey 07621

Please send me the books I have checked above. I am enclosing $_____
(please add $1.00 to this order to cover postage and handling). Send check or money order—no cash or C.O.D.'s. Prices and numbers are subject to change without notice.

Name _____

Address_____

City_____State_____Zip Code_____

Allow 4-6 weeks for delivery.
This offer is subject to withdrawal without notice.